I0692319

THE PSYCHS OF MANHATTAN

A PSYCHOLOGICAL THRILLER

A novel

By C.C. Harris

Publisher: Melissa Graziani
Address of publisher: Queensland, Australia

ISBN: 978-0-6480343-0-8

Cover design and interior formatting by Tugboat Design

CONTENTS

PROLOGUE

The nights were the worst and Joel paced with intrusive thoughts. Emotionally and physically depressed, he feared the dark and had difficulty sleeping. His lack of sleep exacerbated his already low mood and he was consumed by feelings of emptiness.

Now, leaving his apartment in the early morning, he was looking forward to his counseling session and was grateful for the connection with his psych, which filled a void in his life. His psych offered him a safe place, a place where he didn't hide his true feelings.

Joel had been sexually abused by his stepfather since he was eight years old. When his mother had told him to shut his mouth or they'd be homeless, he believed the world would be a better place without him. At fifteen, he left school and ran away from home.

He made friends who'd also had disturbed childhoods. Getting arrested for drug use and stealing was common. Prison ended up being their home, which further screwed up their minds.

Joel had survived life on the streets until he'd found a job and a place to live. Although his past abuse had scarred him, he was no longer trapped in a vicious cycle of depression. He had a psych who cared and didn't charge for his counseling sessions but best of all, his psych gave him permission to cry.

In his first few sessions with the psych, he didn't feel entitled to have therapy, especially as there were others who were far worse off. He also feared his psych would think he was weird. Joel had laughed out of nervousness and minimized his story when he first spoke to the psych. He'd said, 'I'm ok. I survived it. I'm not going to be weak about it and cry. I have to be strong and get over it.'

Now, things were different, as bottling up feelings was something of the past. He stopped burning and punching himself. He knew that if it hadn't been for his psych, he would've killed himself. Joel couldn't imagine life without him.

This morning they were going to do something different. His psych was taking Joel on a walk through Central Park for cognitive environment therapy.

Joel arrived at his psych's office at 9.00 am.

'Hi Joel, I'm glad you could make it,' his psych said reassuringly. 'If you don't want to do this I quite understand. It's not easy trying new strategies to manage anxiety.'

Joel didn't want him thinking he was a quitter. 'I'll be fine. You know I love nature anyway, so it can't be that hard.'

The psych said, 'We can take the elevator to the basement garage where there's a quick access to Madison Avenue.'

The elevator took less than ten seconds to descend and its doors opened to the eerie basement. The sound of dripping water echoed off the walls as Joel inhaled the moldy odors. A chill ran up his spine.

Joel turned to face his psych but there was something wrong. He froze with fear. His cell fell to the ground.

He felt the blade of a knife on his neck.

'What are you doing? I don't want to die, please don't hurt me.' Joel's words were barely audible, blurred by his sobbing. Now he was gulping for breath.

'I can hear that you hyperventilate when you're scared, Joel. Some people just don't understand this world and unfortunately, you're one of them. Remember what we've discussed, Joel? Life is a journey. You are going to experience exactly that.

You're going on a trip to be a special gift to a close friend of mine. He likes boys. Look on the positive side, Joel, your therapy has finished, and you have achieved your goal. You've let go of your fear and trusted the process. You reached your true potential and self-actualized. Well done, Joel,' he laughed.

Joel's world began to spin, and he collapsed as he realized the sinister reality.

A van was waiting with its doors open. The psych placed Joel in a metal box recessed into the floor of the van. There were enough holes in the box to keep his client alive until he reached his destination. The doctor gave a signal and the van disappeared up the ramp and out of sight.

Easy job, the psych thought smugly. No cameras, no one around, and easy access to the van.

He considered himself the best hunter in New York. It was a similar feeling to winning poker. His adrenalin surged as he enjoyed the thrill. Another client outsourced, another contract completed. Today he was going to celebrate his success and enjoy a well-deserved lunch.

ONE

BITE OF REALITY

I struggled to understand how I'd managed to ruin my life because of one bad decision. My client's money had disappeared and so had my penthouse apartment, yearly vacations, and entry to the best restaurants.

I'd risked everything to make millions and rub shoulders with Wall Street's bigwigs.

It all began with my colleague, Jimmy Martin. Jimmy was the top financier in the firm and he had the largest office, boasting a panoramic view of Lower Manhattan and the harbor. His success was nauseating. Don't get me wrong, I was earning a comfortable income, but comfortable meant boredom. I was bored with my job and bored with myself. Boredom was killing me.

I'd decided to invest the Russian mafia's dirty money in a biotech company that seemed rock solid. They'd offered me cash in hand as a bonus, so I couldn't resist. With some creative accounting I covered up their identity, and even invested my own money in what I was told was a sure winner. I'd felt a buzz dreaming of the millions I was going to make.

How wrong I was! Two months later, the biotech company director was found cooking the books and he disappeared, along with his company's money. Not only had I lost my money, I'd also lost $400,000 of the mafia's money.

To make matters worse, the investment I'd picked wasn't in penny shares. It'd taken me weeks to research the company. In the end, no amount of research could have provided information on the ethics of a director. The director is now declared missing with a few extra million in his pocket, and I am declared running for my life. Fuckin' bastard.

In my childhood, the parents of my Russian buddies had worn their fingers to the bone to give their kids a better life. Their doors were open to anyone who wanted to share their family's Sunday lunch and a swig of vodka. I couldn't understand why I'd taken the risk and associated with the one percent of Russians who were thugs conducting community terrorism. I knew one thing. I wouldn't be invited anytime soon to their family lunch.

Jimmy's words rotated like a razor in my gut. 'Curtis... correct me if I'm wrong. Rumor has it you made a deal with the devil and lost. I've heard the Russians are coming, and they're coming for you.'

'I didn't make any deal; the director stole his company's money. He gave himself a nice retirement package and... skipped the country.' There was nothing else I could say to the slimy asshole without sounding like a complete dropkick. I felt like a child facing the school principal and justifying insolent behavior.

He gave me a last verbal souvenir. 'Good luck...keeping alive. They've survived a violent history and they have a ruthless leader. Brutality is in their genes so don't expect them to email you a friendly reminder. From what I've heard, the Russian's dirty money is synonymous with America's political corruption and they're back to using nerve agents they like to call fertilizer. I wouldn't stick around here. You've lost the wrong guy's money, Curtis. Sorry...wish I could help.'

Fuckin' asshole. Why did he state the obvious and give me some fuckin' history lesson? What a dick. As if I didn't know.

But he was right. I knew I was a dead man walking.

The partner of the firm called me into his office. He locked the door and handed me a bottle of bourbon and a gun along with ammo. It seemed he cared, until he told me to get the fuck out of his office before they all got killed.

I had to get out of Wall Street fast. With a gun in my briefcase and hugging my laptop, I ran to my apartment in record time, entering it as if I was robbing the joint. 'Shit, shit, shit!' I yelled as I ran from room to room and stuffed as much as I could into a gym bag. I grabbed a knife and my bourbon. I was running for the door when I suddenly froze. 'Jesus, my cell charger!' I dashed back to my bedroom, ripped the charger from the wall plug, and bolted from the apartment, slamming the door on my privileged world.

I waited at the elevator, pacing back and forth. It was the longest wait of my life. I heard it approach and hid behind the slightly open stairwell door. As the elevator doors opened, my fear was justified.

'What's his apartment number?'

'He lives at the end in 418.'

'We'd better do this job right or we'll be shark bait.'

As they disappeared, I jumped into the elevator.

Once the doors closed, I realized the elevator was going up. 'Fuck no!'

The elevator reached the top floor and then descended. I was gradually pushed towards the back as people entered from several floors. I was sure my desperation was visible as the elevator approached my floor. Sweat trickled down my back as the doors opened on my floor. I was a sitting duck. Jesus, whacked in an elevator. This was not how I wanted my life to end.

The two men entered and turned to face the doors. One was dumpy and looked like he should be running a Russian food store, and the other was tall and skinny. They didn't match their sophisticated suits. *Fuckin' sewer rats,* I thought.

Once the elevator doors opened to the lobby, they walked out, none the wiser.

Calling the cops was not an option. Money laundering and insider trading would give me a first-class ticket to prison.

I jumped on a bus to Brooklyn, which gave me enough time to ring several landlords advertising apartment rentals.

I was in luck. One landlord gave me immediate tenancy if I had a week's cash up front. I guessed the apartment wasn't flash.

Poverty was the very thing I feared and yet here I was heading for some dingy one-bedroom apartment in Brooklyn. My day had started with a relaxed hot shower, the usual cup of coffee, and checking my emails. It ended escaping hitmen and wondering why the fuck I'd dealt with the Russians.

Fifty minutes later, the bus was on Lewis Avenue. I gazed out the window knowing I'd lost everything in the absence of a stock market crash. My finances sucked dry by a company rogue.

The bus screeched to a halt. I stood up, hoping I'd wake up from some crazy nightmare, but instead I heard a voice yell, 'Don't just stand there! Are you getting off or not?'

I reluctantly left the bus and walked onto Lewis. It was only a minute's walk to the apartment block.

Inside, a middle-aged woman approached.

'You Curtis Carter?'

'That's me.'

'I need one week's rent. My husband will see you later to discuss your rental agreement.'

I handed over the rent and took the keys.

TWO

DEATH WISH

As I opened the apartment door, I was welcomed by yellowish-brown walls. It looked and smelt like a public restroom. I collapsed on the bed with my bourbon.

Nothing made sense. My thoughts were foggy, and I imagined crawling into a dark hole.

I'd taken a risk and the red flag had been flying high. I'd totally fucked things up.

As I loaded my gun, I thought how easy it would be to kill the feeling. That way, the Russians would be off my back and I wouldn't have to keep running. Suicide was an easy solution.

The probability of killing myself was a nine out of ten, ten being the trip to the local morgue.

I imagined the pop of a gun and the pieces of my intellect hanging off the wall while a cop yelled at his rookies, 'Hurry up with the body bag! I've got dinner tonight at the Sheraton!'

I pushed the barrel to the roof of my mouth and felt its coolness resting on my tongue, but I couldn't pull the trigger.

I laughed at my dilemma, a laugh that bordered on a cry. I didn't have the guts to extinguish myself. Being a coward saved my life. Killing the feeling was one thing but killing myself wasn't going to happen.

I'd given up smoking years before but now the thought of

a cigarette was irresistible. I didn't give a fuck about my lungs. My form of self-harm was in a packet.

After smoking and staring at the ceiling for an hour, I managed to crawl off the bed. Standing up was an effort.

Emails and messages were constantly beeping on my cell: from a former colleague, the dry cleaner's, an update on the latest trading, and confirmation of my restaurant bookings for the month.

I turned on the shower and leaned forward until my head was immersed under the cool spray. My life had turned to shit, and I felt like shit. Time stood still until I heard a thumping on the apartment door.

'Open up! It's the apartment manager!' a voice yelled.

'Coming!' The last thing I needed was to piss this guy off.

I opened the door to see an overhanging beer gut and bits of food on a scraggy moustache.

'Yes?' I asked.

'What the fuck happened to you? Why are you in a suit and dripping wet? You better not be doing any weird stuff in this apartment or you can get the fuck out.'

'You see...I...um...sleepwalk and this time I ended up in the shower.'

His expression was fixed as his stubby finger pointed at my chest. 'I don't want any problems around here. I manage this place and it's a shithole, so I don't need any more shits to deal with. Got it?'

'Sure. I understand,' I replied.

'I want one month's rent in advance by the end of the week or you're out.'

It was a relief to see the fat man waddle off. He looked like a heart attack waiting to happen. As I closed the door, a roach scuttled across the wall.

I had to find work, and fast. This guy would be in my face again if I didn't cough up the cash. He had my balls in a vice.

I changed my clothes, strapped my gun to my ankle, grabbed my cell and laptop, and escaped my roach palace. It was already 4.00 pm and I was hungry as hell.

Walking along Lewis, everyone looked suspicious, from the newspaper vendor to the little old lady stooped over with a walking stick. I trusted no one and suspected everyone. I headed for the nearest diner. At least Brooklyn had plenty of places to eat and the food was cheap. The chilly day gripped my neck. I pulled up my coat collar and joined Brooklyn's pace.

Walking the streets brought back memories. My parents had worked in the local church when I was a kid and they had helped the homeless. They were compassionate, the ideal community role models. I could still hear my mom's voice: 'Curtis, if you're kind to others the good spirits will be kind to you.'

I'd been a shithead, so any spiritual power around the universe wasn't going to tap me on the shoulder too soon. I wondered why I didn't possess my mom's kindness. My moral compass was non-existent. *Are my actions being jabbed with a sharp syringe called payback?*

To survive, I had to be mindful of every noise, sight, and smell. I was no longer on a dinner invite but on a mafia hit list.

I soon found a diner on Lewis with Wi-Fi. It gave me a chance to grab a bite to eat and search for jobs. I also scanned the latest news. The headlines read: 'Drug doping in sport'; 'Politicians offshore money laundering and secret bank accounts.' *Life could be worse*, I thought. *My name could be exposed. 'Wall Street financier, Curtis Carter, suspected of insider trading and money laundering for the Russian mafia.'*

Feeling temporarily relieved, I searched for jobs online, made a few phone calls, and scored two job interviews. It was then a pretty waitress caught my eye. I resisted a smile. I didn't need anyone. I only had enough energy to keep myself alive.

Looking outside, I noticed it was already getting dark. Although this place looked ok by day, I didn't want to risk walking at night. I gulped down the coffee, tucked my laptop under my arm, and reluctantly left the safety of my booth.

THREE

DISSONANCE

People were hurrying home and vendors were packing up their stores. I bought a couple of packs of cigarettes and a lighter. Sucking on a cigarette felt like heaven. A week ago, I couldn't understand how people worked boring nine-to-five jobs but now, I would do anything to be in their shoes.

It took ten minutes to reach my apartment block. I noticed a figure in the distance wearing a grey overcoat, his arms outstretched. As I approached him, he called out, 'Please help me, I beg you! They're going to kill my friend! Please hurry.' Reeking of alcohol, he pointed a nicotine-stained finger towards a darkened alleyway.

'She's down there. You must help her. Please...save my friend!'

I wondered whether liquor had fucked up his brain and he was hallucinating. For one thing, I wasn't his rescuer and for another, I wasn't going to get killed for anyone.

'What's going on?' I asked.

'Please help me! You must help!'

'I'll call 911.'

'You must help her now! Hurry! Hurry or they'll kill her!' the vagrant yelled.

I was pissed. There were plenty of people standing by. Why

pick me? Did I have 'The Rescuer' tattooed on my forehead? One day I'm trading thousands of dollars' worth of shares and stocks, the next I'm in Shitsville Lane helping some fuckin' vagrant.

I reluctantly peered into the darkness. It screamed of danger. *What the hell, life can't get much worse.*

I dropped my cigarette and squashed the remains with the tip of my shoe. I wasn't in any hurry to get killed. I edged along a brick wall charcoaled with graffiti that depicted a king's crown, praying I wouldn't need my gun. The putrid smell of a dumpster made me gag. I continued forward, stepping around sludge. I reached the corner and slowly peeked around it.

In the alley, I could see three teenage thugs holding a rope. They were suspending a dog, three feet off the ground by its neck. The dog's torso quivered, its paws frantically paddling.

I stepped out from the shadows. 'Let the dog go!'

'Oh, who do we have here?' Like a pack of hyenas, the kids snarled. 'What are you going to do, Mr Office Guy? Maybe we should hook you up too,' the leader laughed. 'Or perhaps you'd prefer my knife? Maybe we could carve you up into small pieces like a pig on a spit.' He waved his knife in the air.

I held up my pistol with my finger gently resting on the trigger. 'What about I blow your head off you fucker.'

'Oh shit, he's got a piece.' The leader of the pack dropped the dog.

'Fuck off now or your head will be a fuckin' soccer ball.'

The leader tripped forward in his frantic attempt to retreat.

The beggar scooped up his dog. 'It's ok Molly, you're safe now.'

I couldn't believe I'd just saved a fuckin' dog. I hated dogs.

'Thank you, thank you,' said the vagrant

'It's all good.' I was a liar. It wasn't good. It was likely these street punks lived here and this was their territory. If word got out that some foreign crazy-ass was walking around with a gun, I was a goner, especially if they were wannabe gang members. Just over a fuckin' dog and some idiot kids with shit for brains.

I gave the vagrant a pack of cigarettes and my lighter. Now I was totally pissed. Giving away my lighter meant buying another one before heading to my apartment. I hoped a part of me cared. A part of me that possessed my parents' kindness.

It wasn't long until I was at my apartment. Once in my room, I lit a cigarette and collapsed on the bed. This was my palace. An apartment with three pieces of furniture, a bed, a small round table, and a chair. The hours drifted by while I smoked, drank, and slept.

I woke next morning to the sound of traffic and crashing metal. I bolted upright in a sweat, still fully dressed, like a deer in headlights. It took a few seconds to remember where I was. A garbage truck screeched down Lewis, intermittently stopping and starting while hooking up trash cans. I imagined a body being hurled into its metal jaws.

The morning presented a depressing start. Raindrops squiggled down the room's dirty windowpane and birds enjoyed a meet and greet on its ledge.

I didn't understand how I'd worked for fifteen years and ended up with nothing. *Does that make me a pathetic loser?* My thoughts were punishing.

I had two job interviews, one as a salesman for a life insurance company, and another as a personal assistant for a psychologist. Both jobs sounded boring, but I was desperate. I had an unexpected flashback, hearing the voice of my grade seven teacher, Mrs Hobbs. 'Curtis, do you know what happens to kids who aren't conscientious at school and who get bored? They want to have fun and fun gets you nowhere, Curtis. Fun doesn't get you a good job and fun doesn't lead to future happiness. Your score for conscientiousness, is pretty much a one out of ten Curtis. That means you never listen, you never pay attention, and you're the class clown. You're destined to be a dropout and ending up in no man's land.'

I remembered Mrs Hobb's long sharp manicured nails. She was better known as Mrs Velociraptor. It was rumored in the school, she transformed into a dinosaur by night and enjoyed slashing the throats of children with one strike of her fingernail. It sounded farfetched at the time, but as a kid, I'd always double-checked that doors and windows were locked at night before bed time. I knew one thing. She was the ten out of ten for being the school bully and making my school days as boring as bat shit. I'd sweat with the sound of her monotonous droning. School was an academic straightjacket of pure torture.

Thank God, she can't see me now.

FOUR

THE INTERVIEW

By 10.30 am, I was running for a bus with a resume in one hand and my cell in the other. My first job interview was at the insurance company situated in the Upper East Side on Park Avenue, less than an hour's bus trip from Brooklyn. The company building boasted a marble foyer. I caught an express elevator to the thirteenth floor, hoping I didn't look desperate.

The elevator doors opened onto a maze of cubicles. People were working in a crammed space only big enough for a desk and a chair. Sitting on windowsills were dying pot plants and faded stuffed toys.

'Excuse me, Sir, did you want to see someone?'

The receptionist had a squeaky voice, as if she had inhaled helium.

I'd been hoping to walk away without her noticing me. I was on the run from doing time, so I wasn't going to be working in an office that simulated a prison.

It was an effort to turn around. 'No, I've come to the wrong place.'

'Don't worry, I've been working here for two years and I still get lost.'

Her high-pitched giggle was painful. I winced. It was a relief to get out of the building.

The second job interview was working for a high-profile psychologist as a personal assistant on Madison Avenue. It sounded easy enough. I had experience in finance, bookings, and meetings. Surely it couldn't be that difficult.

It was an easy walk and I had time to grab a coffee on the way. A coffee was still affordable. I reached the building and took a deep breath. I had to get this job. If I fucked this up, it meant sleeping in the subway.

A flight of stairs led me to a one-person office on the third floor. It seemed ideal. I tapped a bell on a vacant desk. An office door opened.

'Hello, I'm Dr Ellison, and you are...?'

'My name is Curtis, Curtis Carter. I'm here for the personal assistant interview.'

'Ah yes, nice to meet you, Curtis. Come into my office and make yourself comfortable.'

As I entered his room, I noticed a fish tank that ran along the length of his office wall and a silk palm standing in a corner. A black chair faced a cream couch. It looked luxurious. This guy had more furniture in his office than I had in my apartment.

'Did you find it difficult to get here, Curtis?'

'Not at all. Just a quick bus trip from Brooklyn. I like your office.'

'Thank you. I try to create a restful ambience for my clients. Their heightened levels of anxiety can be alleviated by a visually calming environment. My colleague, Dr Lee Cameron, is a psychiatrist. He works on the fifth floor and has his own personal assistant. So, Curtis, take a seat and tell me about yourself?'

Oh crap. What was I going to say? *By the way, I'm running away from the mafia who want me dead. I have no money and I carry a gun.* This guy was a psychologist and I was already feeling paranoid that he could read my mind. Then I remembered a heavyweight stockholder, Harry Hamlin, who'd been around the traps when I was crawling in diapers. He'd pulled me aside and said, 'Curtis, the problem with you is that you're too fuckin' honest. Just fake it until you make it.'

Harry was right, and I'd done plenty of training in speaking bullshit. 'I'd like to...well...study psychology and possibly be a psychologist one day so I thought it would be a good idea to work in such an organization first.'

'That's great you have a plan and some positive goals, Curtis. What do you think I do?'

'You help people.'

'Yes, that's right. I help people, but I need an assistant who can help me run my practice, so I can help people. Does that make sense?'

'Absolutely.'

There was an unsettling feeling about this guy, but I needed the job. His face was expressionless. He gazed at my fudged resume.

'You sound like the person I'm looking for. When can you start?'

'Straightaway.'

'Sounds good to me. You can start tomorrow at 8.30 am sharp. I have client appointments starting at 9.00 am. The appointment book is on the reception desk. I'll run through procedures with you in the morning.'

'Thank you, Doctor, but there's one thing.'

'Yes, Curtis?'

'I was wondering if...if I could have four weeks' pay in advance? I'm helping out my sick mom and finances are tough for her.'

I was sure he knew I was lying. It sounded so fuckin' corny.

'I'd be happy to help you out, Curtis. Give me your bank account details tomorrow and I'll organize a money transfer.'

The guy didn't sound too bad after all. Having the apartment manager off my back was an instant relief.

I noticed a group of stone symbols on his desk as I was leaving.

'You like those, Curtis?'

'Yes, they're interesting,' I replied.

The doc hadn't missed what I'd thought was a discreet observation. I reminded myself that his job was observing people's behavior and that I'd better not fuck up.

'They're Chinese symbols,' he said.

'Do they have a meaning?' I asked, trying to sound interested.

'They mean power and strength.' His response was sharp.

I thought it was strange that someone who helped others seemed so detached.

I was careful not to hang around too long. 'You have interesting possessions, Doctor. Thank you for giving me the opportunity to work for you.' I gave a quick handshake.

Once out of sight, I punched the air, feeling as if I'd just sold stock at triple the price. *I did it!* Now I had to get back to my apartment safely.

On the relaxing bus ride, I remembered his expensive looking patent shoes. They were not from the local Walmart. *Maybe a rich family.*

When I got off the bus, I likened my existence to being in a jungle. My enemy was a mountain cat camouflaged amongst the buildings, waiting to pounce and grip its claws around my neck. I imagined razor-sharp teeth crunching my bones. Crazy thoughts. I needed to turn them off. I bought a bottle of bourbon and a burger, a much-needed pleasure.

Watching the price of stocks was exciting, going out to dinner with business partners was necessary, but imagining someone following me, scared me shitless. The feeling was not unlike childhood nightmares of Egyptian mummies following me. There was no escape, nowhere to hide. Whether mafia or mummies, the fear was the same. My paranoid thoughts continued their stranglehold. *Do I need to walk different ways home to avoid anyone following?*

It was a relief to see my building. Only a minute more and I could collapse on my bed.

FIVE

OCCUPATIONAL IDENTITY

Sassy Lee was a streetwalker who frequented Lewis Avenue. She had been working the streets since she was seventeen and now at twenty-three, she felt comfortable in this part of Brooklyn. Sassy knew how to plant the seed of sex in a male's brain for lustful germination. Her clients were slaves to their addiction. She knew sex was no different from heroin, providing a fix for their cravings.

Sassy was street smart. She had plenty of repeat customers. Pretending she enjoyed the sex brought them back. It was one of the first tricks of the trade.

She made them pay up front because once they'd finished with their business transaction, clients were reluctant to part with their cash.

She worked for a pimp who didn't slap her around and demand sex. He allocated a few streets to her that she claimed as her own. She was street smart with the customers. The dangerous clients were those who offered fame and fortune. The naivety of the young streetwalkers made them a vulnerable target for customers who had a lust for torture and snuff movies.

She could still hear the last words of her friend: 'Oh my God Sassy, I have this amazing offer. I met this guy who said he's a big movie producer. He said I've got what it takes to make it and I was special, just like my mamma told me. He's offered me a modeling photo shoot and a movie deal.'

Sassy had pleaded with her not to go. Crystal just gave an affectionate laugh and said it was nice someone cared but not to worry, she would text her after the shoot. That was the last time Sassy saw or heard from Crystal. She didn't get a text. She simply vanished off the face of the earth.

Sassy knew the warning signs. If a client pulled up in a cargo van, truck or anything else that could keep an unsuspecting victim captive, she knew to stay away. The prostitutes who were hooked on drugs and desperate for a quick fix took their chances.

She remembered a lucky escape when she first hit the streets. A middle-aged guy who looked like he was on his way to a Woodstock Festival offered her a weekend away. He said he was going camping and had some amazing weed that he didn't mind sharing.

Sassy felt trapped in the city and yearned for the country air. She couldn't resist. She'd smoked some weed in her time, so she was looking forward to escaping her world for the weekend. He looked harmless enough, even showing her pictures of his kids.

Just as they were leaving the city, she noticed a knife, rope, and duct tape on the back seat. Her survival instincts kicked in. In sheer panic, she opened her door and jumped.

Her skin along the lower part of her body was scraped off and she heard the crunch of bones as she bounced along the interstate. Sassy escaped but she ended up in hospital with a bloodied and battered body.

She didn't think too much about it again until the police caught up with her months later. She identified the mugshot of a man who was known as the Highway Hippy Killer. He preyed on prostitutes, runaways, and hitchhikers. Now, he was sitting on death row. The police told her she wouldn't have made it if her killer had had automatic locks on his vehicle doors. Hearing the words 'lucky to escape' traumatized her more than the experience. It gave her shivers to think of the torture he would've enjoyed. It was another thing in her life that made her feel stupid and worthless.

Now she didn't work without a taser. She serviced a retired cop who gave her the tools and the knowledge to protect herself. Sassy found him different from most clients. He cared about her safety. No one was interested in the good cops; it was always the bad cops that sold newspapers. The usual headline was: *A crooked cop, a prostitute, and dirty money.*

Sassy lived in a small, one-bedroom apartment in Brooklyn and she was fortunate to have some regular clients. She had a six-year-old daughter who lived with her parents. Working on the streets gave her enough money to put her daughter through school. She considered visiting her daughter was better than her daughter witnessing her mom's loser life.

Sassy was the queen of disassociation and consciously split her personality to survive. On the streets, she was Sassy, and off the streets, she was Sandra, a caring mom who would do anything for her kid.

She didn't remember having had a happy childhood. As a teenager, the longer she'd stayed at school the dumber and more depressed she'd felt. Her self-esteem was non-existent and the cuts on her arms were a cry for help. She enjoyed being with like-minded friends couch surfing and not having a care in the world. They spent most days getting high. One day, she jumped over the school fence and never returned.

After one of her drug highs, she fell pregnant. She didn't know who the father was. Her mom begged her to stay home to raise her child. Sassy felt alienated from others in their small town. She couldn't bear to stay at home, in a place that produced small minds, so she packed her bags and kissed her baby goodbye.

Her life changed in a flash when, alone and hungry at New York's central bus depot, a pimp picked up her bags, fed her, and bought her clothes. Before long, she was working the streets and pulling in more cash than she had ever dreamed of. She sent cards and money home for the baby and pretended she had an office job.

Although Sassy's pimp looked after her, for some time she had wanted to turn her life around and start again. The job brought too many risks and she didn't want her child to lose her mom. Sassy knew she had been in denial of the seediness of some of her clients.

She was finding it harder to put up with clients whose sexual fantasies made her feel physically ill. One client had whispered in her ear, 'We are going to play a game because you are special. Suck your thumb and call me Daddy while I touch you and stroke your princess hair, but don't tell Mommy. This is our little secret.'

Now she wanted to find her true self and be a positive role model for her daughter. She enrolled in a business degree and was ready to celebrate her new identity. Today was going to be the last time she stood on a corner. She finally had the courage to tell her parents the truth about her life. She had enough money saved for her studies and she could afford to see a psych for career counseling at The Manhattan Well-being Clinic.

SIX

CRYSTALS AND NIGHTMARES

'What about it, cutie? I can give you fifteen minutes any way you like for eighty dollars.'

I jumped, ready to reach for my gun. 'Jesus, you scared the crap out of me,' I said.

'Sorry I scared you, I'm sweet Sassy.'

'All good,' I replied, my pulse racing.

One look at Sassy and my breath quickened. I was starved for sex and here was an opportunity to escape my loser reality even if it was a momentary fix. Instant satisfaction had been my downfall in the past and I didn't dare look back now. The last thing I needed was to feel like shit on top of my self-loathing. I made a beeline for my apartment block before my dick ruled my brain.

The longest relationship I'd ever had was with fiery Maria Chianti. She had offered me a burning passion for life and great sex until one night, I'd ended up in a drunken state between the legs of someone else. Maria had hurled my clothes off our balcony and screamed, 'You're just an arrogant, self-entitled pig! You don't care about anyone only yourself. One day you'll look in the mirror and know exactly what it feels like. What you've done to me will come back one day and bite you. It'll be your karma!'

What frightened me the most was that Maria's words were ringing true.

In my apartment, I stood by the window. I had a bird's eye view of the street below. A shadowy figure was standing against a bus shelter. As the figure looked up, I ducked out of sight.

Was he watching me? Had he been hired to sculpture my skull with bullets, a 1940's-type hitman waiting to fulfil a contract and fatten his bank account?

I pulled down the blind. I'd been careful. I'd told no one where I was staying. Collapsing on the bed with my pistol resting on my lap, I listened to a hungry mouse scavenging for food and a couple fuckin' in the apartment across the hall. I drifted off to sleep, my dreams haunted by sights of blood and death.

My grandmother called my dreams a hereditary gift from her people that I needed to embrace. 'You have the power to help others, Curtis. You're connected to our lost people and that means you can see things that others can't. Curtis...open your mind...you will see the world differently.'

My family ancestors are Native American. I glanced at a tribal tattoo stretched across my arm and felt a pang of guilt for not honoring my people. I wondered why I heard punishing voices. Why people were always making me feel guilty. Persecuting me. Telling me how to fuckin' live.

I'd felt my eyes droop when suddenly I jolted forward. I was sitting on a train. What the fuck was I doing on a train. Passengers had gaping wounds. I looked away, repulsed, and choked on the sweet odor of rotting flesh.

'Where the fuck are we going?' I yelled.

A fleshless skull half turned. 'We've finished our journey; we are going nowhere.'

'What...what the hell do you mean?'

'This is your destination. There's no more stops. You're at the end of the line.'

My legs were paralyzed. Passengers reached out to touch

me. The windows and doors were locked. I was trapped. Buzzing sounds became louder and louder. I brushed a fly from my ear and looked up. The ceiling was in motion and looked like rolling waves. A mass of flies covered its surface. The feeling of overwhelming fear and the stench of death were suffocating. I gasped for air and tried to yell, but nothing came out. My legs still wouldn't move.

A passenger reached out with her bony fingers. Her blonde hair was matted with blood and on her finger, was a crystal ring.

'Please help, don't let him take me. Please, I know you can help,' she begged.

A sea of arms tugged at my clothes.

My eyes flashed open. My bed was a pool of sweat. I looked at the walls half expecting them to move as I resisted the urge to vomit. It was a familiar nightmare: people begging for help. It was draining. I just wanted everyone to piss off. I did a mad dash to the bathroom and patted cool water on my face, then hung onto the edge of the basin to catch my breath. My life was fucked and so were my dreams. As far as I was concerned, dreams had no meaning and the whole thing was bullshit, although the smell of death was up my nose.

Trapped on a fuckin' train swarming with flies and talking with mangled bodies left me feeling lightheaded and nauseated. I glanced at the clock. It was 6.00 am and I felt as if I'd just run a marathon. Fear was fuckin' exhausting. I hoped I wasn't destined to some fuckin' mental ward. My door labelled 'Crazy Curtis.'

As I reached for my shaver I heard a noise. As I turned around I saw a mouse running along the skirting board. Jesus Christ, I was sharing my apartment with a fuckin' mouse. The mouse suddenly stopped and looked up as if I was the intruder. 'I can see you're wanting to get out of this shithole. Well bad luck. You'll have to make the most of your accommodation.

You're stuck here with me but be grateful you're not in a mouse trap. In the meantime, no playing or sleeping on my bed. You got it?'

His whiskers twitched disinterestedly, and he groomed himself, unperturbed by my conversation.

'You look like a Charlie that doesn't give a shit about us fuckin' humans. If you're good, you'll get a few scraps tonight. I usually don't like rodents but...for now...you can live. Just make sure you stay out of my way. It's the first day of my job.' I pointed my shaver in his direction hoping for a response, but there wasn't a single squeak. 'If only my enemies were your size Charlie, life would be easier.'

Glancing around the apartment before leaving, I thought again what a stark contrast it was to my former apartment.

As I hopped on a bus to Madison Avenue, my thoughts drifted to the mystery man of last night at the bus shelter. A reminder that I had to pay off the mafia fast.

The bus arrived on Madison just in time. As I entered the building, I wished I could spend the day under the trees in Central Park watching baseball.

My first morning at work was busy. Clients came in for appointments all day and the administration tasks were straightforward. The doctor was either good at his job or there were lots of wealthy people who thought they needed help.

It was 4.00 pm and the doctor's last client for the day was Courtney Williams, waiting patiently and flicking through a magazine. Something caught my eye. My glance became a stare.

'Is everything ok?' she asked. She had a sweet, soft voice.

'Oh yes, sure, it's just that...I couldn't help noticing your ring. I like it, it's very...unusual.'

'Oh, thank you. It's a crystal. I fell in love with it as soon as I saw it. A Chinese vendor said that he had lots of rings but this one was...somewhat special.'

'Why did he say it was special?' I asked.

'He said the ring had chosen me. The crystal deflects negative energy. Sorry, I hope I haven't gone on too much.'

'Oh no, not at all. Anyway, I'm the one who asked.' I gave her a reassuring smile. It was the ring from my dream. I wondered at the chance of seeing the same ring the very next day.

My thoughts were interrupted by a light flashing on the switchboard. It was the doctor.

I pressed the button. 'Yes, Doctor?'

'Could you send Ms Williams in please?'

'Sure,' I responded.

'As this is my last client, you can finish up for the day, Curtis.'

'Thanks, Doctor. See you tomorrow.'

I caught an express bus to Lewis. Once in Brooklyn, I headed out for a pizza. *Brooklyn isn't so bad after all,* I thought. Something about the place gave me a sense of freedom, the same feeling I'd had growing up. As a kid, I'd roamed around my neighborhood without a care in the world, sometimes on my own and sometimes with friends. Life had been simple. *How had it got so fuckin' complicated?*

My thoughts drifted back to the client's ring and I wondered about the creepy coincidence. I thought it weird that people relied on inanimate objects to change their lives. I wished I wasn't so cynical. I wished I believed in something that was empowering.

It was easy to find a pizza bar and the pizza was the best I'd tasted. Before leaving, I grabbed a piece for Charlie.

Back at my apartment, I watched Charlie nibble at his dinner and hoped the Russians weren't coming.

SEVEN

MINDFULNESS

Before Courtney started seeing a psych, she didn't think her life could change. Her income came from working on the streets and pleasing her pimp.

Courtney suffered guilt over rejecting her family, who were devout Catholics. At the age of twenty, she'd got caught up in the drug scene and before long, prostitution and drug dealing were part of her daily survival. In the end, she hated herself and hated the sex industry.

She received a morsel of money compared to her pimp. Despite the thousands of dollars that changed hands, she still lived in public housing on the Lower East Side of Manhattan, where the rats were the size of cats. She'd slept with corporate leaders to seal business deals and it wasn't unusual for her pimp to place a hidden camera during sex romps for blackmailing clients. The clients were easy prey.

Courtney missed her hometown and especially her younger sisters. She had no contact with anyone from her past as she couldn't bear them knowing about her life. When clients were scarce, she lived off food stamps and visited the local soup kitchen or YWCA. To Courtney, the Lower East Side was a place of loneliness and her heightened intuition sensed the presence of lost and displaced souls from another time.

Courtney's only friend had ended up hanging from the end of a rope after her ex-boyfriend had posted her nude selfie on-line. That night, Courtney had felt as if she was stranded on a desolate island. She felt invisible to the world. A ghost that people looked through as if she didn't exist. Nothing seemed to matter.

Her feelings of loneliness were overwhelming, and her reality became scrambled with suicidal thoughts. Courtney's negative emotions escalated after she diagnosed herself online as having a major depressive disorder. She feared she would never be fixed. She couldn't see the point of living if she was always going to be sad and lonely. She had decided it was the only way out. No one would care if she was gone. She came to the realization that life didn't make sense.

She remembered the sound of a distant train. She was standing still and quiet on the platform, staring at the railway track as the train approached. *I wouldn't feel like a failure anymore. It would be easy,* she thought. She wouldn't feel a thing. All she had to do was step to the edge and jump. She had made up her mind she didn't belong. She was nothing and nobody cared. The forgotten one. This was her ticket to freedom from intolerable pain.

Then, as she stood on the platform edge, she heard a voice. A voice that was calm and soothing and that didn't judge her. *'Please step back and stand with me. I want you to be safe. I will help you.'* She didn't see anyone, and the next thing she remembered was waking up in the Manhattan Psychiatric Centre and spending two weeks undergoing a personalized therapy program.

Her suicide plan had failed but she noticed she didn't feel so hopeless and the voices in her head were no longer persecuting. The warmth of that stranger's voice on the night of her suicide plan stayed with her. A voice that cared whether she lived or died. A voice that was by her side on the platform.

She walked away from the hospital afraid she'd relapse, so she decided to follow through with a mental health plan and see a therapist. She was fortunate enough to see a psych who advertised free consults at her local YWCA. She had weekly sessions and enjoyed the bus trip from the Lower East Side to the world of the privileged in the Upper East Side.

Courtney liked the contrast between New York's haves and have-nots. It motivated her to better herself. She wondered how her psych could counsel others when he lived a privileged life free from financial stress, until he disclosed to her a childhood of suffering and pain. She saw him as her role model. Someone who could make positive changes despite the odds. His self-disclosed traumatic childhood made her feel a deep connection with him. He understood her. He knew what it was like to struggle with adversity. She had at last found what she longed for. Her soulmate.

During this time, an inheritance investigator tracked her down to a soup kitchen close to her apartment and left his number. At first, she thought it was a joke or her old pimp looking for her. To her shock, when she called the number, she realized the investigator was genuine. She had hardly known her grandmother but for some reason, she had cared enough about Courtney to leave her a Ford Focus and some cash. *Had her grandmother been the voice at the train station?*

She moved to a better part of New York and underwent drug and alcohol rehab, continuing her weekly counseling sessions with her psych. She was determined to stay away from drugs, and she wanted to continue with the counseling until she felt safe enough to cope on her own. She knew if she didn't resist the drugs, her life would be finished.

Courtney stopped working on the streets and found a part-time job at her local convenience store. She considered it her first real job. She liked her boss and enjoyed the contact with customers. For the first time in her life she'd felt worthwhile. She was no longer consumed by feelings of hopelessness. One day she hoped to study social work and help others. She couldn't believe how her life had turned around.

Courtney looked out of the doctor's window and noticed it was getting dark. She had been talking with her psych for over an hour and now she was wondering why her counseling session had gone well over time. She didn't want to be traveling home in the dark. At times, she found it difficult to be assertive. The last thing she wanted was to offend him. She looked at her watch and gathered the courage to speak. She stood up and hooked the strap of her bag over her shoulder. 'Thank you for the session but...I must get going.'

'Next week then Courtney, same time?' the doctor asked.

'Yes, that would be great,' she responded as she walked towards the elevator.

The doctor caught up and pressed the elevator button. 'I'll escort you down to the basement garage, it provides a quicker access to Madison. Oh, and here's the book I promised. It's about healing the mind and the body.'

'Thank you. It looks like a useful resource.'

He must think I'm special, she thought, amazed by his kindness. One day she would repay him. She couldn't imagine him being absent from her life.

She flicked through the book's pages as the elevator descended and wondered why he cared so much while others had rejected her.

'Thanks again for the book.'

'You're welcome Courtney. I'm glad to offer any resources that will be helpful.'

As the elevator doors opened, she stepped into the dimly lit basement and could see the access to Madison Avenue.

'I appreciate you escorting me, but I'll be fine now. I can see the exit.'

'Bye Courtney, have a safe journey home.'

'I will.'

As she walked away from the elevator doors, she turned to give her psych a wave but to her surprise, he was already gone. She didn't want to miss her bus, so she quickened her pace. She thought she heard a noise. She stopped to listen and quickly scanned the basement. Nothing. *That's strange,* she thought.

She challenged her catastrophizing thoughts just as her psych had taught her and repeated positive self-statements. 'I'm ok, I'm safe, there's no one here.' As she walked towards the exit, she heard the noise again. This time it was louder. This time she realized it wasn't her catastrophizing thoughts. Her heart was pounding, and she was trembling. Panicked, she felt her throat tighten and her breathing became restricted.

'Who's there?' Her voice echoed through the basement and off the unforgiving walls. There was no response.

Her inner voice told her to run but she was paralyzed. The book slipped from her hands. It was too late. She was grabbed from behind. Her body was violently jerked backwards, and her heels scraped along the ground. She caught a glimpse of her attacker as he pulled her hair. She had trusted him! He'd been caring and supportive. *How could he do this? How could this be happening to me?* she thought.

'Why?' she asked. Her voice was barely audible. 'You said... you said I was a good person and I was special.'

His words were mocking. 'You know, Courtney, bad things happen to good people. I'm sorry my dear, I'm not your knight in shining armor but I will tell you a little secret. Your fun is about to begin.'

She was at his mercy. She heard voices and a vehicle screeching through the basement. She hoped the voices would save her. She gasped. *Is this my punishment from God? Is this my fault?*

'Please...please...I beg you...let me go...I don't want to die.'

'Don't you remember, Courtney? Happiness is valuing the

present,' the doctor said with a sinister laugh.

Her life flashed before her eyes, and she knew it was the end.

He pitilessly dragged her fragile body to a waiting van. She tugged on her finger and her crystal ring fell onto the basement floor. She hoped someone would find it. She prayed he hadn't noticed.

She heard his last chilling words.

'Thank you, Courtney. We've had a positive and collaborative relationship, but now you are my financial solution. Because of you, I'm $700,000 richer. Financial mindfulness is such a wonderful thing. Enjoy your journey Courtney and remember, live in the moment.'

Only seconds later, she realized she was in a moving van.

* * *

How easy it had been to obtain her trust. He praised himself. All the fools in the world working shit jobs with shit pay while I'll be rich.

The abduction excited him. He wished she'd been his for the killing, but he was getting big money for her safe delivery. He smiled at his handiwork and picked up his book. *What a clever time waster,* he thought. The book had served its purpose well. He felt the rush of adrenalin as he recalled her bewildered expression. Having the power to control his victim's destiny was euphoric. Another exhilarating image surfaced from his memory, that of his stepbrother's distorted face as he fell to his death. He no longer felt impotent.

He felt like a God again.

EIGHT

PAST LIAISONS

My apartment stank of mold, and the water pipes creaked. The room had a depressing chill. Life in the diner was preferable. If it was open twenty-four seven, I'd still be there. I watched Charlie nibble on his treat and then I drifted off into a deep sleep that brought no nightmares.

The next morning, I bought a coffee on my way to work and ducked into the work basement garage for a puff. The basement reminded me of my apartment, cold and dreary. I hadn't even got to the cigarette when I heard a voice close behind me.

'Hi Curtis, how are you this morning?'

I jumped with fright. 'Good...thanks.'

'What brings you down to the basement, Curtis?'

I pulled out the cigarette from my pocket and held it up. 'Just having a quick cigarette...you know...a quick puff before the day starts.'

I wasn't sure where my boss had come from. He'd been so quiet. I felt like a loser, a nicotine desperado.

'There is one thing, Curtis. I'd rather you didn't talk to the clients. I overheard the conversation between you and Courtney Williams. You see, my clients can experience delusional thoughts and exhibit disturbed and problematic behaviors.

It's important that the less said the better, for the sake of their well-being and yours. Do you understand me, Curtis?'

I felt like a scolded child. I really wanted to tell him to fuck off, but I needed the job. I paused, maybe long enough for him to notice I was holding back my true thoughts.

'Certainly Doctor, it won't happen again,' I responded with feigned sincerity.

I hated feeling powerless. Already this guy was giving me the creeps. I wondered how much of the conversation with Courtney he had heard and why he cared about my well-being.

The doctor's eyes were cold, and his authoritarian demeanor was unsettling. As I watched him walk away, something caught my eye. It was a ring. Courtney's ring. *What the hell. How did it end up here?* As I bent down to take a closer look, the doctor suddenly turned.

'Is everything ok, Curtis?'

Jesus. Did the guy have eyes in the back of his fuckin' head? 'Yes. All good.' I pretended to fasten my shoelace as I carefully edged my shoe on top of the ring. As he turned back to walk on, I scooped it up. *Why was Courtney's ring in the basement?*

When the day was done, and I was heading down Lewis again, twirling the ring in my hand and looking forward to a bourbon, I heard the rev of a car. I glanced discreetly to my left. A vehicle was following me. I quickened my pace and then bolted, instinctively.

'Police! Freeze!'

This was crazy. What did they want from me? What the fuck was I doing? Was my brain telling me I was a dead man if I stopped? It took me seconds to hurdle a bus bench. I flew around the nearest corner and straight into the arms of a cop. My head thumped against the gutter and a knee ground into my back.

'What do we have here? You usually walk around with a revolver strapped to your leg?'

'I haven't hurt anyone. What the fuck's going on? You can't arrest me!'

I tasted blood trickling from the corner of my mouth. I felt woozy and standing up wasn't easy. He handcuffed me and forcefully pushed my head down, shoving me into the back of a patrol car.

'Hi Curtis, it's been a long time.'

Jesus, it was an old colleague, Sarah Wilkins, sitting in the back seat! We had worked together as realtors more than eight years before. When the property market hit a slump, the buyers had dried up along with our commissions. Tired of waiting for weekend buyers, I'd got a job at the brokerage firm on Wall Street and clawed my way up the ladder to become a financier. The last thing I remembered about Sarah was a call from her telling me she was working in New York as a security officer. How the hell did she go from being a fuckin' security officer to a top cop of Brooklyn? Her petite figure and black hair drawn back into a neat bun didn't fit a tough cop image.

'Was this your idea of kicks, Sarah? Why do you need to arrest me like some hardened criminal?'

'You're behind the times, Curtis. Where have you been hiding? Didn't you hear? I'm a detective lieutenant working for the NYPD. When there's trouble I take it personally. I'm committed to public safety.'

'Don't give me that bullshit speech about bloody safety! Fuckin' hell. We did the same job not so long ago. Remember? And I don't need to hide out, Miss Personality of the NYPD. I was just walking home when your guys decided to jump me. I thought you had more class than to wind up being a cop. You really surprise me, Sarah, working for a corrupt force like this. I've heard about the NYPD. Money passing around in brown paper bags. Good cops turning into bad cops but still thinking they're the good guys. Don't give me this "I'm better than you" crap, Miss Goodie Two Shoes.'

'Have you finished your little rant, Curtis? You know that's bullshit. We've always got Internal Affairs breathing down our necks like bloody sniffer dogs. My team work around the clock. Like any job, there's the risk of a bad apple and besides, statistics show that the crime rate has dropped but you won't hear that. Why is it always assumed there's money floating around in bags?' Sarah gave a sardonic chuckle. 'That sounds so clichéd, Curtis. I think you've been watching too many movies or you believe the media myths,' she said, taking a knowing swipe at my self-esteem.

'It's lovely to hear your sharing and caring Sarah. I really enjoy being lectured by a woman, it really makes my fuckin' day.'

'I do my job and look after my boys, so I don't give a shit what you think about the force or me, Curtis. What I do care about is that you've been working on Wall Street, but there's a few missing pages in your life.'

'What's it your business and why am I getting the sense that you're accusing me of something whilst enjoying your moment of power, Miss Good Cop?'

'We have a killer on the loose.'

'Well, it's not me...anyway, what's so unusual about that? I'm sure there are plenty of killers in New York keeping you busy.'

'We've been keeping an eye on a couple of prime suspects, and that's where I recognized a familiar name. That familiar name being you. You're working at The Manhattan Well-being Clinic for a psychologist, Doctor Ellison, right?'

'Well I'm not working for Jack the Ripper,' I quipped sarcastically.

Sarah paused and raised her eyebrows.

'I'm telling you now there's no way the doctor is a killer. It's just...well...it's just not possible.'

'Give me a good reason why not,' Sarah said.

'Because he's not only a psychologist, he's a doctor and

doctors help people and because...I don't want him to be. I'm just getting my feet on the ground and I need the cash. If I lose this job, I'm stuffed. The last thing I want is to be involved in some half-assed cold-case investigation. I was feeling good until you lot showed up. Jesus, talk about buzzkill.'

'Who said it was cold?' Sarah responded.

'Well he's not killing now...is he?'

'We don't have any evidence yet but some of his clients are ending up dead, or they're listed on our missing persons database. And what astounds me is that a prostitute called Sassy Lee was found dead in a dumpster not far from your apartment. Is her name familiar?'

'This is fuckin' ridiculous. What would I know about a murdered prostitute?'

'Her parents said she'd been working the streets and her real name was Sandra. And you wouldn't guess where she was going for counseling. The Manhattan Well-being Clinic.'

'Look, I've just started working there. Anyway, he has a colleague, Dr Lee Cameron on the fifth floor. How do you know it's not him?'

'Don't worry, we're checking him out too. They could be working together. And what's this ring we found in your pocket? Are you ready to propose, or is there something more sinister going on?'

'Haha, very funny. I found it in my work basement this morning. It belongs to Courtney Williams, a client of the doctor's. She must have dropped it after her counseling session. Honest to God...I'm no killer for Christ's sake...you should know me well enough to know that.' I knew I could be in trouble. She was talking about a killer and I had a client's ring.

'Now I want you to listen very carefully, Curtis. The commissioner has put up a $500,000 reward to catch this guy.'

'Why is the commissioner so interested in this case?' I asked.

'Confidentially, his niece Linda Maloney was found dead a year ago, at Lake Mead in Boulder City, mutilated from head to toe. It was nasty. She'd been tortured. The only evidence we have is a pair of eyeglasses found next to the body. They could belong to the killer because the commissioner's niece didn't wear glasses and they're male designer glasses. We've been tight-lipped about the murder. The public don't know the victim was the commissioner's niece and we have no idea how she ended up at Lake Mead, thirty minutes from Vegas. If the media get hold of this, all hell will break loose. The case is in the deep freeze until we have enough evidence for an arrest.'

'Why so secretive?'

'His niece was troubled. Long story short, she was a runaway. She was cooking up crystal meth and dealing on the streets. The commissioner doesn't want his family's dirty laundry aired, especially anything involving drug dealing. The elections are coming up and he wants to look squeaky clean. He's a crusader against drugs.'

'And let me guess, the commissioner's niece was seeing my boss, Doctor Ellison, would that be right?'

'Very perceptive, Curtis. That's right.'

I wasn't sure whether she was having another swipe at my self-esteem.

'Where do I come into this so-called plan of yours?' I asked.

Sarah's voice softened. 'We need your help.'

I couldn't believe how quickly her tone changed from accusatory to sucking up.

'After you've just roughed me up like some hardened criminal? You've got to be kidding!'

'Sorry about that.' She sounded sincere, but I wasn't convinced. 'Well you see, Curtis, you're what we call our lucky break.'

'What do you mean by lucky break?' I asked.

'What I mean is, we need you to...um...maybe go undercover?'

'What the fuck? I help you and then I end up...what...dead! Screw that.'

'You'd be safe, Curtis.'

I knew that an informer was usually the first to get a bullet to the head.

'So now I'm supposed to feel safe after hearing this?'

'We would never put you at risk, Curtis. You'd be under twenty-four-hour surveillance. Your every move would be monitored. Of course, it's up to you but I assure you that if we get this guy, the police commissioner will cough up the reward.'

Her offer sounded enticing. She was dangling the sweetest carrot. 'How much of the reward do I get?' I asked.

'If we nail this guy, you get a cool $500,000 guaranteed and signed off by the commissioner himself. By the way, sorry for roughing you up. My boys didn't know why you were being arrested. I'm trying to keep the lid on this case until I get my team together.'

'If I say yes, will you give me my gun back?'

'Ok, it's a deal.' Sarah signaled to a rookie who was out of earshot. He looked more like a 1960's street punk than a cop. 'Give him the gun.'

It was a relief to have it back.

'Well then, when do I start?' I asked.

NINE

REJECTION SENSITIVELY

Brandy locked her front door and threw her bag down on the entrance table. She lived alone in a house that was cheap to rent and close to transport. Living by herself had its advantages as she hated people watching her twenty-four seven and calling 911 when she cut herself. She liked to think she didn't need anyone's help, but there was a part of her that wondered why she was so lonely.

Throughout her school years, Brandy had been bullied relentlessly on social media and called a slut. Kids laughed at her and told her the world would be a better place if she killed herself.

Her feelings of abandonment supported her world view that no one loved her, and she might as well be dead. She wondered how many people would care if she killed herself. In retaliation, she externalized her depression by lashing out and blaming others. Brandy began binge drinking every other weekend and habitually relaxed by smoking weed.

She'd left home at eighteen, as her mom couldn't cope with her mood swings and angry outbursts. She felt her mom minimized her emotional pain when she called her a drama queen.

She lived with various friends, but they soon grew tired of her unpredictable and erratic behavior, which included several attempts to end her life. They eventually told her to leave. She knew that her mental health was a drain on others and was relieved to be on her own. Despite this, she couldn't help but feel isolated and angry. The more she demanded love and attention, the more her friends disengaged from her. Boyfriends didn't last more than a month. They too grew tired of her demands and temper tantrums.

Mrs Harper was a neighbor who lived across the street. She was retired and often visited Brandy for a chat or delivered her a home-cooked meal. Mrs Harper's husband had died several years earlier, and she was the one person who didn't judge her and especially didn't ask about the scars on her arm. From her bedroom window, Brandy noticed Mrs Harper's light was on. She was sure she would soon be visiting with a meal.

Her thoughts drifted to her psych. She had been seeing him for six months and was looking forward to her appointment tomorrow. She travelled an hour to New York once a week for her therapy.

He was the first person who'd truly understood her. She could talk about her provocative behavior, angry outbursts, and attention seeking without him judging her. Her therapist was the father figure she had always wanted, and this attachment kept her alive. There was no one else who listened and validated her like he did. *He was different,* she thought. *He wasn't like the rest. She could trust him. He was dependable and faultless.* She knew she would be safe if he was there to support her. She no longer felt empty inside.

One day, Brandy hoped to write a book about well-being. A book that showed the world her life struggles and how she had survived her past traumas. She wanted people to understand how much pain she had suffered and how unique her life had been.

As Brandy turned on the TV, she noticed a text message from her psych saying their appointment the next day was canceled. She felt a surge of anger. *Surely if he really cared he would make me his priority.* She couldn't understand why he would abandon her when he knew she was suicidal.

'Nobody's issues could be more important than mine,' she protested aloud as her self-harming impulses took over.

Her self-deprecating thoughts escalated to verbal ranting: 'No one gives a shit. They all leave me. I can't depend on anyone to help. My family, friends, the nurses, and now my therapist! They expect me to take my antidepressants like I'm some fuckin' psycho. They're all useless. No one cares that I feel like crap.'

She clenched her fist, wanting to punch the wall, but instead took a razor from her bathroom cabinet and rolled back her sleeve. She made a small incision across her wrist. Her overwhelming feelings of anger dissipated as she watched the color red trickle into her palm.

She knew not to cut too deeply. She didn't want to end up in hospital. She hated hospitals; they made her feel like shit. The medical staff always dismissed her and treated her meanly. She could hear their singsong voices: 'Here we go again, another attention-seeking borderline wasting our time and resources.' Her psych, on the other hand, soothed her anger and told her she was not attention seeking but seeking the attention she had a right to receive. Now she wondered why he wasn't going to be there for her tomorrow.

She dabbed antiseptic on her cut to prevent infection and placed enough pressure on her wound to stop the bleeding. Her breathing slowed as her body relaxed. She grabbed a bandage and wrapped it around her wrist. She threw on a long-sleeved top to cover the wound, so Mrs Harper wouldn't notice.

As Brandy finished wiping the blood from the basin edge, she felt uneasy, not from her wound but from a gut feeling that something was wrong. She could smell cologne. She recognized the familiar fragrance but dismissed her senses as delusional.

Instead, she reminded herself of her psych's advice to challenge her irrational thoughts. 'It's ok, I'm overthinking...I am imagining it...I am safe...' she said aloud.

As she looked in the mirror, she remembered a time when she had thought that mirrors were windows. Now she realized how crazy that thought was. Brandy studied her tired eyes, noticing the greyness of her skin and the dullness of her long black hair. Although she was only twenty-three, she felt twice her age. The years of emotional pain had taken their toll and now, her therapist had canceled her appointment. She wondered whether she was the only one in the world who felt like this.

Then, she was no longer focused on her reflection. She looked beyond her face. She wasn't sure... What had she seen? She held her breath. Her body froze. Her peripheral vision detected a movement. *What was behind her? Was the reflection an illusion?*

She knew she had locked the doors. Her chest heaved with fear. Her thoughts raced as she retraced her steps. She had come home, locked the front door. It was impossible for anyone to get in. Now she wondered whether she had forgotten to lock the back door in her rush to leave the house that morning. The bottle of antiseptic slipped from her grasp as she turned to face him. She wanted to scream.

'Hello Brandy, you're late tonight. I've been waiting for you. You really should remember to lock your back door. I wasn't expecting to just walk in. Thank you for making it easy for me.'

Her legs turned to jelly, and she gasped in fright.

'Why...why are you here?'

'It's ok, my darling Brandy. You won't feel a thing.'

She stared into the eyes of a sadist whose acts of kindness had just been a façade.

'I...I...don't understand,' Brandy stammered. 'You read Romans...Romans 12:9 and told me to...to let love be genuine.

"Abhor what is evil and hold fast to what is good." My love for you was genuine and I...I...held on to your every word. I thought you cared.'

'Brandy, Brandy...the clever ones hide behind the words of God to indulge in their true delights. But that is our little secret. The reality of your sad life is that no one cares about you. Look on the bright side. Your life is no longer meaningless. You are special to me. Now you have a purpose.'

He stepped forward and jabbed her in the arm with a needle.

A dose of tranquilizers surged through her body. She rocked from side to side until she fell into his arms. *As light as a feather,* he thought.

'You were right, Brandy. You do freeze, my darling. It goes to show you have to be careful what you tell people, especially someone you trust.'

He had planned her abduction meticulously, staying hidden in the dark by her house, watching and waiting for the right moment to strike. His vehicle was nearby, ready for her easy transportation. He knew she would never guess her fate. That was what he enjoyed the most.

Anticipating the hunt and watching the horror and disbelief in his victim's eyes.

TEN

ENJOYING THE MOMENT

Mrs Harper was worried. It was most unusual to see Brandy's light on and her drapes not drawn, so she didn't hesitate to go and check on her. Within a minute, she was at Brandy's front door.

'Brandy...Brandy...are you there? It's Mrs Harper...your neighbor.'

Shit, the neighbor, he cursed. He knew he would have to kill her if she saw him. He clenched his fists. Not delivering Brandy would cost him a cool $700,000 and he knew his buyer would be pissed.

The doctor picked up Brandy's blade, unwrapped her bandage, and sliced her wrists downward, severing a vein. He then placed the blade in her hands. *No one will suspect foul play*, he thought. She was a self-harmer with the habit of going to hospital.

Fuckin' nosy neighbor, he thought. He wanted to kill her, but it would make the job too messy. Things had changed. Brandy had seen him, and he wasn't willing to stare at four walls for the rest of his life or be strapped to an electric chair to fry. The only consolation was he had a backup plan. His plan was a syringe of heroin that he kept taped under his driver's seat. If necessary, he would eliminate her at the hospital. The police wouldn't suspect a thing.

Mrs Harper peered through several windows until she spotted Brandy's legs on the bathroom floor. She immediately called 911 and ran to the back door. She was surprised to see it open. Little did Mrs Harper know that she was inches away from a killer. A killer who was standing hidden behind the back door as she rushed to Brandy's side.

When the ambulance arrived, he watched patiently from the comfort of his vehicle until the ambulance headed to the Hospital. He followed closely behind and parked at a distance from the hospital, taking the syringe from under his seat. *You're a genius Luke. Keeping this heroin has paid off.*

He waited for an hour, hoping it was enough time for her to be transferred to the intensive care unit. Waiting too long heightened the chance of her gaining consciousness.

He didn't risk ringing the hospital, instead accessing the ward from the stairwell. The doctor knew hospitals were generally understaffed and security was slack, especially around stairwells. He also knew if she wasn't in the ICU it was going to be a headache finding her.

Once in the ICU, the doctor glanced down the hallway. The nurses' station was unattended. It was visiting time, so he wouldn't stand out. Nurses glared at kids running in and out of rooms, and families paced impatiently at the nurses' desk. Perfect. It was a busy night and there were no police or security in sight.

It wasn't until he peeped in the third room he noticed a drape drawn. As he stepped forward, he felt an adrenalin rush. He pulled the drape aside to see Brandy attached to a heart monitor. *Fuckin' bitch, she survived,* he cursed inwardly.

He was tempted to put the syringe in the drip line but that wouldn't be quick enough. Once he was by her bed, he took the syringe from his pocket and removed the cap. He gently pulled back the sheet and quickly scanned her arm. Once he'd found a vein, he injected the ultra-pure heroin.

As he stood watching, Brandy's eyes unexpectedly opened, staring at him terror-stricken. He couldn't help but return the stare and enjoy the moment. He knew it could be a quick death and couldn't resist staying until her blood stopped circulating and her heart collapsed.

As he recapped the syringe and placed it in his pocket, he thought how smart he was to choose such an empowering career. The career of a psych. He leaned over her bed and removed his gloves. 'You were the one who wished to be dead, Brandy,' he whispered. 'Remember Brandy, happiness is a state of mind. It's your journey that counts, not your destination.'

Before he left the room, he smirked with pleasure. 'You have wonderful insight, Brandy. You were right. You were a bad girl and you deserve to be punished.'

ELEVEN

MISSING PERSONS

Sarah called me dead on 8.00 am.

'Hi Sarah, you're an early bird. Ready to catch the psychopath, are you?'

'Why the hell don't you answer your cell, Curtis? I've been trying to call you!'

'Saturday means sleeping in...anyway, what's so urgent that it can't wait? Don't tell me...the White House has blown up?'

'Not funny, Curtis. I've got bad news. We have another victim. Her name is Brandy Johnson. She died last night at the hospital.'

'Jesus, already?' I responded.

Sarah sounded breathless. Her anxiety was contagious.

'You said the crystal ring you found in the basement garage belongs to Courtney Williams, the psychologist's client.'

'That's right,' I said.

'Her boss called us as she hadn't turned up for work. Her boss said this was out of character. He said he'd tried to call her several times but there was no answer. We tracked down her parents. They said she'd left home a couple of years ago and they didn't know where she lived or what she was doing. Anything planned for this morning, Curtis?'

'By the sound of it I'll be seeing you,' I answered.

'I'll have someone pick you up.'

'Sounds good to me,' I replied.

Once at the precinct, I was greeted by a colleague of Sarah's.

'Curtis, I'd like you to meet James Christianson. James is a criminal psychologist I've pulled out of retirement,' Sarah said.

'Hi Curtis,' he said with a firm handshake.

'Nice to meet you,' I lied. I could see the headlines. *Criminal psychologist pulled out of retirement, helps catch serial killer. A hero's funeral for Curtis Carter, who sadly didn't survive.* I wondered whether Sarah liked me or if I was just a useful tool to solve a case.

'Thanks for coming, James. How was the trip?' Sarah asked.

'When a helicopter arrives at my front door, I know this isn't any ordinary case. Besides, golf was getting boring; there are only so many holes you can play.'

Sarah led us to a debrief room that was an ideal place for cabin fever.

'Right, what have you got for us?' James asked Sarah.

'We have a serial killer or serial killers and our suspects are Dr Luke Ellison who is a psychologist and Dr Lee Cameron is a psychiatrist. They have a business called The Manhattan Well-being Clinic. Curtis is currently working for Dr Ellison, as his personal assistant.'

James and Sarah gave me a stare. I felt like the sidekick who knew fuck-all about investigations. Maybe I'd have been better sleeping under a bridge in front of a communal fire pit.

Sarah produced a file on the table. 'The victims on our books include a prostitute called Sandra. Her street name was Sassy Lee. She was found dead from a heroin overdose, but she wasn't a drug user and she'd been to The Manhattan Well-being Clinic the week she was murdered. We also have Brandy Johnson who was also having therapy at the Well-being Clinic. She died in hospital last night. That means Sandra and Brandy are dead and Courtney is missing. Doctor Ellison's and Doctor

Cameron's work numbers came up on their phone records.'

Sarah took a deep breath. 'The victims lived on their own, they had no friends and no contact with family members. They were all younger than twenty-five and of a similar height and weight – no taller than five feet two. They'd be easily overpowered. One of the victims was the commissioner's niece, Linda Maloney. Her body was found a half an hour from Vegas. She was attending The Manhattan Psychiatric Centre because of her previous suicide attempts and drug use.'

'Do you think the doctors know we're on to them?' I asked.

'Not a chance. We're known as the covert chameleons of New York.' Sarah grinned. 'Dr Ellison lives alone in a condo overlooking Central Park. His colleague lives on his own on 85th Street. I don't have enough evidence yet, so I don't want to spook them, or they could disappear.'

The meeting reminded me of my school days. I'd break out in a sweat trying to sit still. Luckily, I had a chair that swiveled three hundred and sixty degrees.

Sarah rolled her eyes. 'Curtis, really. Can't you keep still?'

'It's not easy,' I replied with a grin.

'Just wondering James, is there a term for a lack of focus?' I asked.

'Yes. Maladaptive daydreaming disorder.'

Sarah looked up from her paperwork. 'Are we here for therapy, or what?'

'Sorry,' I said.

James straightened his posture. 'The offenders are well organized with their abductions and choose their victims carefully. The victims are high-risk as the community are not going to give a rat's ass about missing clients who have a history of suicide attempts. The clients would've been an easy target, especially if they'd trusted their therapist and felt safe.'

Sarah placed her hand on James' arm. 'It's great you can help us, James.'

It was hard listening to her gratitude with James. I was the one who should've been thanked. I was the one going into the fuckin' lion's den.

'Why do you find this case so special?' James asked.

Sarah smiled. 'Usually I'm relieved if I don't have to work on such a serious case, my team are stretched as it is, but I want to get this son of a bitch off the streets and I'm hoping for a good reference from the commissioner. I'd like to work in California.'

'I thought you enjoyed living in New York and getting the bad guys,' I said, hoping not to sound too concerned.

'I'm feeling burnt out and I don't want to end up a wreck. I'm already struggling to sleep more than four hours a night. I'd like to live on the coast. I can't think of anything better than beach walks. Anyway, enough about me, I'd better brief my team and get onto the paperwork. I can drop you home before the brief if you like, Curtis?'

'Thanks, but I'm good.' Truthfully, I wanted to take *her* home and have a day between the sheets.

'Thanks for your help Curtis. I really do appreciate it,' Sarah stated.

I felt like a school kid with my hands in my pockets waiting for my first kiss. I needed to think with my head and not with my dick. If I needed sex, I could pay for it, with no strings attached. Anyway, I knew women liked me. I could have anyone if I wanted. *Love is for fools,* I thought.

'Happy to help if it means putting some psychopath away.' I was full of shit. I had to get the reward. If I didn't pay off the mafia, I was as good as dead.

TWELVE

TRUST

Janis was enjoying working on her coloring-in book as it provided a world of beautiful colors, shapes, and patterns, replacing the ugliness of her past.

She'd had an unhappy life. Her mom was an alcoholic and a drug user. Living with her had been like walking on eggshells. Tragedy struck when Janis was sixteen. Her father jumped off the Brooklyn Bridge. The day he jumped, she found a leather jacket in her schoolbag with some cash in the pocket. With the gift was a note that read: 'An early Christmas present, love you always, Dad.' Although they barely had enough money, she hadn't thought twice about it until a police officer came knocking at their door.

Christmas and birthdays were the hardest without him. She thought of him every day and couldn't understand why he had gone and left her. She'd sit by her bedroom window, watching and waiting, hoping he'd walk through the front gate. She hoped the cops had got the wrong ID. At times, she thought she could hear her father's voice and she'd dash to the front door to greet him. When she shopped, she'd notice anyone who looked slightly like him.

Several months after his suicide, Janis stopped searching for him, accepting he'd gone. Her inner dialogue relentlessly repeated the same questions: *Why did you want to kill yourself? Didn't you want to stay with me? Did I do something wrong? Why didn't I notice something wasn't right? You seemed so happy that week.*

Janis didn't feel she deserved love. She wished she could cry. Years of feeling trapped because of her mom's neglect stopped the tears and she masked her pain with a fake smile. Some days, her feelings were so overwhelming she couldn't see the difference between killing her pain and killing herself. She just wanted the hurt to stop.

She found it difficult to concentrate at school and regularly saw her school counselor for support. Her pastime was cutting her wrist to deal with her emotional pain. Each time she achieved any academic success, her mom would scream, 'Ya ain't goin' nowhere in life. With all those fuckin' books ya read. Ya think ya better than anyone else. Well ya not. Ya an attention-seeking bitch. Ya good fa nothin' loser. Ya can't even do fuckin' chores ya lazy bitch. I'm fuckin' sick of ya, ya whore!'

It had been difficult not to internalize her mom's words. At home, she lived in her bedroom while her mom continued her drug use. With the help of her school counselor, she stopped cutting and graduated from High School. On that day, she walked away from a life of misery. She kissed a photo of her father and said, 'I'm sorry, Dad. I'm sorry I couldn't save you. I hope you're proud of my graduation.'

She then tucked his photo in the pocket of her jacket and walked out the door. She was a free spirit. Free from the shackles of her mom's psychotic rages. She looked back at her house for the last time and it was then she wondered if her dad had felt the same relief on the day he'd walked away.

She now lived alone in a tiny apartment opposite the Bronx Zoo and worked as a waitress. She'd heard of bad stuff going on in some of the housing projects and stayed clear of them. She soon realized the transport was great and parts of the Bronx were pretty. Janis loved the Southern Boulevard diners and spent her Sunday afternoons people-watching over a coffee. She wasn't sure why the Bronx got such a bad rap, with its beautiful gardens and cheap shopping.

Janis was grateful for her sanity and independence. She knew it didn't matter where someone lived in New York, it didn't stop them from killing themselves. The Brooklyn Bridge didn't discriminate on class when someone wanted to jump.

Although she had a regular job and enjoyed her newfound sense of freedom, the fall-out from her childhood abuse lingered. She noticed an advertisement on her local YWCA noticeboard for free therapy sessions at The Manhattan Well-being Clinic. She decided it was a good idea to see someone about her mental health and before long, she was seeing a psych on Madison Avenue.

She no longer felt pressured to think positively and some days found her living conditions and low mood a reason to change her life for the better. She also had a thirty-year-old stepbrother who had located her and kept in touch. He visited once a week to make sure she had enough food and was safe.

After having therapy at the clinic for some months, her sleeping patterns improved, and she learned strategies to regulate her emotions. Her psych diagnosed her with post-traumatic stress and provided the talking therapy she needed. She considered her psych as her emotional rescuer. He supported her self-esteem and cleared her dark thoughts. Janis knew she could not fix her past but since seeing her psych, she had been able to shift her thoughts from the bad stuff and stop her anxiety and nightmares. He praised her insightful reflections and validated the pain and suffering she had endured as a child.

He told her how proud he was of her emotional resilience and how much she had learned in therapy. Her psych gave her a coloring-in book as part of her relaxation therapy. She'd enjoyed coloring in as a child and now it quietened her bad thoughts and provided a positive distraction.

* * *

But for Janis Lang it was too late. Her killer was already circling her building like a vulture, watching...waiting...ready to swoop.

As Janis sipped her tea, she was alarmed by a knock at the door. She didn't know anyone who knew her address apart from her stepbrother. Who could it be? she wondered. She looked through the peephole in the door and was surprised to see a familiar face. She hesitated. *Why hadn't he called her instead? Why would he come to my apartment? Maybe I'm being paranoid,* she thought.

Dismissing her gut feeling, Janis opened the door. 'Hi Doctor. Is something wrong?' she asked.

'No, not at all. Sorry to disturb you so late. I forgot to tell you I'm going away for a few weeks and I'll have to reschedule our appointments, but I have the voucher for the well-being seminar we had been talking about. As I won't be here I thought I would personally deliver it to you.'

'Oh, thank you. That's kind of you.'

'While I'm here, do you mind if we have a chat about something?'

'Come in. I can make you a tea or coffee if you like?'

As she turned her back, he locked her door and stepped forward, following her closely.

He didn't answer her question.

She suddenly felt a forceful grip around her shoulders. She was in the arms of a monster.

'Remember Janis. I didn't choose you, you chose me to begin your new identity. We worked well together creating your new story. A story from self-defeating beliefs to self-empowerment. For your enthusiasm and curiosity in our narrative sessions, you will be rewarded with a positive consequence. This is the defining moment of your life, my lovely Janis.

Janis had always thought of ending her life but now, someone else was deciding her fate. She switched her thoughts to a faraway place, a place that was safe and calm, disconnected from her terrifying reality.

The doctor clamped the chloroform-soaked cloth over her face. *I'm in control again,* he thought. As the chloroform took effect, he visualized his growing bank account. Her virginity was worth a cool $800,000.

THIRTEEN

PAYBACK

I'd just showered when Sarah rang.

'Yes Sarah, what is it this time?' Little did she know I was standing stark naked wishing I was holding her.

'Hi Curtis, have you heard of a Janis Lang?'

'Yes. She has weekly appointments. From what I can remember she lives on her own.'

'She's been reported missing by her stepbrother. He said she was having counseling on Madison Avenue, but he didn't know who she was seeing. We checked out her apartment and there was no sign of forced entry or a struggle. Her handbag and keys were on the coffee table along with a coloring-in book and pencils. She had money in her bag and there was cash in a jar in the kitchen, so we've ruled out robbery. Looks like she just disappeared into thin air – and quickly.'

'Were there any witnesses?' I asked.

'Neighbors saw and heard nothing. So now we officially have Janis Lang from the Bronx missing. The commissioner's putting the pressure on us to get this guy. It won't be long before the media will be connecting the dots.'

I didn't interrupt. She had given me the worst possible news.

'Curtis, are you still there?'

'Yes...I'm...I'm listening. I'll do a quick snoop around today.

I start work at 9.00 am. Shall we meet today...maybe for lunch?'
I asked.

'No, meeting for lunch is too risky. Give me a call when you
get home after work. You'll have around-the-clock surveillance
starting tomorrow, so keep your head down until then.'

'What's up?' I asked.

'Be careful.'

'You know me Sarah, I'm a survivor. No one's going to get
me. I'll call you after work.'

Sarah's call left me feeling edgy. A noise from outside my
room suddenly made me jump. Charlie skittered across the
floor in fright. I held my breath. My brain went into autopilot.
Wrapping a towel around my waist, I edged towards the door.
Suddenly the door handle rotated. *Jesus, someone was trying
to get in! Oh fuck, oh shit. I realized I'd left the pistol under my
pillow.* Too late. The door burst open with such force that my
head slammed against the wall. I felt a fist in my stomach and a
blow to my face. I hit the ground face first.

Someone grabbed my hair. My head was violently jerked
back. I looked up to see a killer with a tattoo of a double-edged
dagger on his neck.

'Where's our money, you fuckin' asshole?'

'I'm getting your money. Jesus...can't you see where I live?
I'm trying...I'm trying to earn a buck to repay you. You will get
your money...I promise.'

'You have two weeks to cough up $400,000. If we don't
get our money, we'll be back to get you. You can't escape the
Russian dagger! Do you understand asshole?'

I managed to grunt a yes.

'Here's another reminder we mean business, svoloch!'

This time I got a full-strength kick to my side.

I don't know how long I was on the floor, but I knew I had
to get to work. I dialed the only person who could help. 'Sarah.
I'm sorry but...I'm wondering...um...whether you have...um...

any makeup to cover a few small bruises, and some pain-killers?'

'Small bruises? Aren't you off to work? We were only just talking.'

'I just need a quick make-over.'

'For God's sake, Curtis, what's going on? You're doing my head in.'

'I'm sorry Sarah. I've just been a little...sort of...roughed up but I'll explain when you get here.'

Sarah arrived with makeup and painkillers in one hand and a coffee in the other.

'Here's something to help the pain. Now rest back on the chair so I can see this messed-up face of yours.'

'Thanks. You're a life-saver.' This time I meant it.

'What have you gotten yourself into, Curtis?'

'I invested the Russian Mafia's money in a biotech company. Unfortunately, I fucked up. The director of the company took off with his company's money along with mine and the mafia's.'

'So you're desperate for the commissioner's reward,' Sarah said.

'You could say that. My bank balance isn't looking good.'

'I hate to tell you this, Curtis but...um...between us...Brooklyn is where the Russian crime boss lives. He owns a Russian tea room in Brighton Beach and operates a crime syndicate. I can't give you any further information, it's pretty much classified, but probably a good idea not to dine out in Brighton. There is one other thing.'

'Tell me,' I replied.

'I've heard the boss's mom has a kind side. If she likes you, then she'll waive your debt and you'll live to see another day. If she doesn't, then say your prayers.'

'Jesus! That would be right. Thanks for the tip. I'll keep that in mind if we meet. Obviously, his mom thinks her son is a good boy. I feel like I'm living in Russia.'

'Well, I thought it was better you know. Now sit still and I'll patch you up.'

I wasn't sure whether I felt good knowing the Russians lived on my doorstep or whether ignorance would've been the better option.

After a few minutes, Sarah had covered my bruises. Looking in the mirror, I tilted my head from side to side. She'd done a great job. I looked almost normal again although I felt like shit.

'You know, Curtis, you can pull out any time. Remember my team is starting twenty-four seven surveillance tomorrow so don't do anything stupid until then.'

'Don't worry. I'll be careful.'

Once Sarah left, I strapped a knife to the lower part of my leg and tucked my gun behind the fridge. I gulped a few pain-killers and checked my cell.

I was at work by 9.00 am.

The doctor messaged he was going to be late, which was perfect. It provided me with the perfect opportunity to snoop around in the basement garage. The run-down basement didn't match the renovated building. It was cold and damp. Birds found their nesting spaces in concrete crevices and a dumpster stood in the far corner, overflowing with trash. There was nothing I could see out of the ordinary. If he was taking his victims to the basement, he didn't leave any evidence that I could see. I hoped Courtney's last moments hadn't been in this hellish looking place.

It was after this thought I felt a hard object press against my head. I knew this could only be one person. Fuck, I couldn't believe it. Everything I touched turned fuckin' dangerous.

'I thought you had more brains, Curtis. You're just a small-time punk. Don't even think about turning around or your brain will be splattered across the ground.'

'What the fuck. I'm having a cigarette and you're pulling a gun on me?'

'Don't think I didn't see you snooping around. If you'd just minded your own business I wouldn't have to do this,' the doctor sneered.

'You're not going to get away with this...you psychotic bastard. You're mentally fucked!'

'Well, well, Curtis...you do get angry, don't you? You know... letting your emotions get the better of you is detrimental to your health. Your heart rate can increase, and you'll want to run. That's what you do best, isn't it Curtis? Continually running away from your problems. It's just occurred to me that with your lack of grey matter, it's difficult for you to make the right decisions. You fuck up, explode, and run off like a little boy. Does that sound somewhat familiar, Curtis? Am I getting close to the true you?'

It was obvious he was enjoying his depraved sense of humor.

'Behind all that verbal bullshit you're nothing, Mr Psychopath Psychologist. Fuck you!'

'There there, Curtis. It's important you don't work yourself into a pointless frenzy. You know, you're nothing but house-keeping. I'm not letting someone like you get in my way. You see, being a psychologist allows me to understand you more than you understand yourself. Your behavior keeps you developmentally stuck. You haven't progressed from adolescence. To put it simply, Curtis, you keep repeating your fuck-ups,' the doctor laughed. 'We could have worked well together, but because of your self-sabotaging habits you have nothing. No occupation, no friends and I would guess no self-esteem.'

'You really think I would team up with a psychopath? One day you'll be kicked off your fantasy throne and onto a chair that will zap you like an insect until you burn from the inside out.'

'I like that, Curtis. You almost sound intelligent but with your highly reactive personality, you're the loser. Don't worry Curtis, you're just like millions of other losers who lack insight. Intelligence is all about adapting to one's environment. Survival of the fittest. Such a shame you fail so superbly in that area. Good luck pushing up daisies. And by the way, someone is taking good care of Courtney and Janis. I'm sure you remember sweet pretty Courtney. I'll leave you with that thought while you say goodbye to this world. A world that doesn't give a shit about you Curtis.'

The last thing I remembered was the sound of a sliding door and feeling a sudden force to the back of my head.

FOURTEEN

NURTURING EVIL

Sarah was pacing. It was 9.00 pm and Curtis hadn't called. She waited an hour then checked his apartment. There was still no sign of him and his calls were going straight to message bank. Courtney, Janis, and now Curtis were missing. She felt sick to the stomach. *Christ Curtis, where are you?*

She was petrified something had gone wrong. Curtis had promised to call after work. Was he lying somewhere injured or in a hospital? Had the doctor found him snooping? Had he taken off, so the mafia couldn't find him, or had they tracked him down? Sarah knew the Russian mafia were in bed with local politicians and bankers. She wondered whether Curtis was incredibly naive to have dealt with them, or just plain stupid.

Sarah returned to the department and gave the bad news to James.

'Thanks for coming, James. I can't believe Curtis has vanished. Hopefully by morning, we'll find something among this pile of files that will give us a lead. Janis from the Bronx, whose dad jumped off the Brooklyn Bridge, is still missing. Her mom told us to fuck off when we rang. She hoped her daughter had killed herself. Courtney, whose ring was found in the basement garage, is also still missing. Her mom couldn't tell us anything about her daughter, only that she'd abandoned God and accepted Satan. Sandra has a little girl who doesn't have a mom, while Brandy is cold at the city morgue.'

'I'll find something on this callous bastard,' James responded.

Sarah didn't often hear James swear but it settled her nerves. She was grateful to have him on the team.

Sarah placed two large boxes of files on the desk. 'Sorry to ruin your retirement, James.'

'Not at all. Who wants to be brain dead in retirement? This will get the brain cells firing again.' James gave a genuine grin.

He didn't let on how much he had missed working. He was glad to be away from golf lunches and boring chitchat. Anyway, he owed Sarah. She had saved his ass years earlier when he'd worked for the NYPD. He'd gone through a relationship break-up and hit the bottle hard, hiding away for several months. Sarah had covered his shifts until he was ready to resurface.

'Curtis was private about his personal life and his parents are no longer alive, but I remember him talking about his brief stint at Fort Jackson. I don't know whether that's clutching at straws.'

'Anything is better than nothing,' James replied as he poured himself a coffee. James called Fort Jackson and the National Personnel Record Centre in St. Louis. He was surprised how quickly the NPRC accessed Curtis's records and how willing they were to fax them to the precinct.

'Well there you go. Faxing isn't dead after all and they even gave me priority to archival information. This proves, it's not what you know but who you work for,' James chuckled as he forwarded a verification of ID by email and waited for the fax.

Sarah was hopeful that Curtis had enough fire in his belly to survive. Before her mind wandered any further the fax came through.

'Jesus that was quick. They've faxed through his report and

from what I can see, he nearly completed his training.'

'What's the go with Fort Jackson?' Sarah asked.

'It's a military training installation that trains in basic combat with hands-on skill development. I'm guessing he wasn't sitting in a classroom note taking.'

'What else is there?'

'Mmm...your Curtis was a naughty boy during his training.'

'That sounds like him,' Sarah mused.

'From what I see his drill sergeant found him swigging bourbon. It states he refused to stand at attention and instead of saluting her, he pissed on her boots. He was consistently confrontational. There was no court martial, but he was given his marching orders.'

It infuriated Sarah that she was attracted to Curtis and that he had dared piss on his sergeant's boots. Now she had evidence of his deviance and lack of basic decency.

James sat back and looked at Sarah. 'Curtis's army record gives us a clue to his personality. It sounds like he was hot headed. His weakness could be the very strength he needs to escape a killer. Let's hope his personality and army training will provide the recipe for his survival.'

Sarah shook her head. 'Serial killing, I just don't get it.'

'I likened it to gold fever. Gold fever provides a dopamine rush not unlike killing,' James replied.

'What about Dr Ellison's personality?' Sarah asked.

'If he has a sense of entitlement, killing can feed into his narcissism.'

'But James, he's a psychologist, wouldn't he know that?'

'He thinks he can psychologically outsmart his clients and the police. He'd be skilled at ingratiating himself with others to manipulate a positive impression. As you'd know, they can be a pallbearer at their victim's funeral.'

'From your past cases James, what have you noticed about a killer's childhood?'

James gazed down at his coffee cup. 'As you know, serial killers are rare but before working for this department I'd interviewed a killer called the snake. He said when he was four years old, he had pinched a boy hard and it felt good. He admitted when the kid cried for his mom he'd hurt him even harder. He said he'd got better as he'd got older and in elementary school he'd set kids up as if they'd been the bully. He said the kids were shit scared of him and kept their mouths shut. He grinned when he'd explained how easy it'd been to lie. He was proud of his craftwork.'

'Were there any other red flags?' Sarah asked.

'He said he'd fed a deformed kitten to the class snake and watched the kitten scream and struggle whilst the snake slowly strangled it. He'd admitted he then went to the school bathroom and ejaculated. I remember him justifying the killing. He'd said the kitten was sick and was going to die anyway. He'd filmed it on his cell, so he could enjoy the thrill of the kill at home.'

'That's sick,' Sarah stated.

'Yeah, you're not wrong,' responded James.

'When did he shift from animal killer to serial killer,' Sarah asked.

'He said when he'd graduated from college, he'd enjoyed being the snake. He said he'd pick up a prostitute and slowly strangle her, savoring the torture whilst ejaculating. Again, he justified his killing by saying that prostitutes were the rejects of society.'

'How did you get him to tell you that?'

'He seemed to have liked my attention and enjoyed telling his story as if he was getting off on it.'

'What about his parents?' Sarah asked.

'They said their son was really sociable but if anyone crossed him he'd deck them.' James looked up, and asked, 'Are you sure you have nothing at all on the doctor?'

'Nothing,' Sarah stated. 'He has no website advertising his practice or his therapies and the FBI's National Database failed to come up with anything. Not even a parking ticket. He's squeaky clean. To make matters worse, I've been asked to write an article for the New York Times on my views of rehab. They'll have to wait.'

James was skeptical of rehab. Rehab meant going back to their former healthy state. He believed psychopaths didn't possess a former healthy state. Their former state was torturing a family pet before their fourth birthday while receiving indulged and permissive nurturance from parents who feared being labeled neglectful and dismissive. Parenting paranoia that produces a ticking time-bomb.

'Where are you Curtis?' Sarah said aloud, not caring that James could hear her desperation.

They worked meticulously through the night on every piece of information, taking power naps and eating pizza.

Sarah sighed. 'I had the commissioner on my back again. He's getting restless and he wants an update.'

Sarah felt like a circus performer, juggling responsibilities to her team, delegating and managing paperwork, keeping the budget on track, and trying to appease the chief, the commissioner, and the media.

The public were ignorant about the lack of resources and the financial constraints. They just wanted answers, and she didn't blame them. At times, the department became a pressure cooker and tempers flared, especially when staff were looking for time off or more pay. Seeing big-time drug dealers driving fancy cars didn't help either.

The worst aspect of the force was cops who were exhausted. It jeopardized the chances of getting a killer off the streets. Their partners had no choice but to tolerate the night shifts or their twenty-four seven call-outs. Every fortnight, Sarah shouted her team a dinner and a few beers at the corner bar. It was a great way to boost morale. She worked out some creative accounting. Bar nights went under the meetings budget, and she didn't hesitate to put her own money on the table for drinks.

Sarah recognized that her sleep was irregular, and the nightmares were increasing. Getting seven hours' sleep was history. Exhausted, her thoughts drifted back to Curtis. She was praying he would suddenly call and laugh it off.

'Gee, time really does fly when you're desperate to solve a case,' Sarah groaned. 'The suns coming up and we're no better off.' She stretched her arms out wide and wriggled her fingers as if she was playing a keyboard. She usually covered her mouth when she yawned, but even this was too much of an effort. Her mouth opened wide as she held her head back and rubbed her eyes.

At that moment, one report jumped out at James. 'Sarah, what's this about professional misconduct?' He slid the folder across the table.

'Jesus...I'd forgotten about that. From what I remember, a client claimed he assaulted her in the basement garage.' Sarah scanned the paperwork. 'Her name is Nancy Fisher. Thanks, James, for your fresh pair of eyes.'

'What's her family background?' James asked.

'Her parents live in Ohio. They said their daughter was diagnosed with factitious disorder, and so there were serious doubts about the accuracy of her complaint and her sense of judgment. Doctor Ellison's license was only temporarily revoked during the investigation. The allegations of professional misconduct were later dropped when she decided not to press charges.'

'Mmm...there is a problem,' James stated. 'It could be a case of the boy who cried wolf. If she was telling the truth, it would be difficult to convince a jury that this time she wasn't lying. I wonder whether the doctor crafted the client's factitious diagnosis. It would be...let's say...a convenient diagnosis.'

Sarah pushed back her chair and picked up her jacket. 'You may have just found the break we've been looking for. How about we check Curtis's apartment again then pay Nancy and her factitious disorder an early morning visit?'

'Good idea,' James responded.

FIFTEEN

COGNITIVE ENVIRONMENT THERAPY

Nancy lived a good forty minutes out of New York. Her front yard looked more like a dust bowl, with weeds growing three feet high around the perimeter of a wire fence. *What a depressing and lonely looking place,* Sarah thought.

Before James had a chance to knock on the door it opened, exposing several chains looped across the gap.

'What do you want?' Nancy asked.

'Hi Nancy, I'm Lieutenant Wilkins and this is my colleague Detective James Christianson. We're from the NYPD and we'd like to ask you a few questions.' Sarah and James flashed their badges.

'How do you know my name?'

'You were one of Dr Ellison's clients, is that correct?'

'Why are you asking?'

'We'd like to talk to you about your complaint against the doctor,' Sarah said.

'I've told the police everything. Sorry...I have to go.'

'We won't take long,' said James.

'I've already gone through hell and back with him. Can I have another look at your badges?'

James held them up again.

Nancy slid open the chains. 'Come into the lounge room.'

Her voice was timid.

She moved papers off a couch. 'I'm not used to visitors. Sorry about the mess.'

'No need to apologize,' Sarah responded.

'My cat Emmy...she really likes company, so excuse her affection.'

'You don't need to worry about that, I love cats,' Sarah said, tickling the cat's neck.

James looked down at the police report. 'We noticed from your complaint that Dr Ellison assaulted you in the basement garage of his building, is that correct?'

Nancy shifted nervously in her chair.

'Take your time. We know this is difficult for you,' James said. He knew he had to be sensitive. She was extremely vulnerable.

Nancy thought they sounded genuine, but she was still guarded. She had trusted her psychologist. Now she trusted no one.

'Why would you believe me? No one else did. Not even my own family believes me,' Nancy responded flatly.

'Because we read your complaint and we believe you. We don't want this psychologist to keep hurting people. Are you able to remember what happened?'

'He said...um...as part of our therapy session we would go... um...for...a walk through Central Park. It wasn't until we got down to the basement that I felt...sort of nervous.' Nancy spoke in a whisper as if the psychologist was listening in.

'Why were you in the basement?' Sarah asked.

'He said the basement provided quick access to Madison Avenue.'

'What happened next?' Sarah asked.

'Once we were in the basement I told him I'd changed my mind. But he became insistent that I try his CET therapy.'

'What exactly was this CET therapy?' Sarah asked.

'Cognitive environment therapy. He said it was like mind-fulness. But he made me promise...'

'What did he make you promise,' James asked. 'No one can hurt you now. It's ok.'

'He made me promise to keep it our secret until it was accepted as a leading therapy for anxiety. I had to sign a confidentiality agreement. He said I had unhealthy perceptions of the world which caused my panic attacks and my brain needed...I think he said...retraining. He said my thoughts needed changing to stop my anxiety. In every session he said I worry too much and I'm severely disturbed.'

'What else did the doctor say?' Sarah asked.

'He said being in Central Park was the ideal place to do his therapy, so I could experience being in the moment with nature. He said I had a critical voice that needed quietening in a peaceful environment. I thought he was so clever. He said he was the first person in the world to discover this ground-breaking therapy.'

Sarah continued her questioning. 'What happened then?'

'At first, what he said made sense. I wanted to stop my anxiety attacks and get off my medication. He knew I hated taking medication. He promised one day that I would be free from drugs. He said he was...really proud of me.' Nancy stammered, then looked up. 'I hope I'm making sense.'

'You're definitely making sense. What happened next?' Sarah asked.

'I told him I wasn't sure and maybe we would do it another day, but he was insistent and said I would never get better. He said I would always hear the negative voices in my head and never be free from medication. I felt guilty for doubting his therapy. Nancy gazed at her feet as if reliving the moment.

'It's ok Nancy. He can't hurt you now,' Sarah stated.

'He put his arm around my shoulders and his voice... changed.'

'What do you mean his voice changed?' James asked.

'He sounded angry. He said he expected more of me and that he was disappointed. He sounded like my dad. I was scared...I was scared he wouldn't see me again. I felt I couldn't live without him. I was ready to agree to the therapy until suddenly...'

'Until suddenly what? I can understand this is very difficult for you Nancy, but no one is going to hurt you.'

Nancy stroked her arm. 'He tightened his grip around my shoulders.'

Sarah continued validating. 'You're doing well, Nancy.'

'Then a maintenance man walked out of the elevator.'

'How do you know it was a maintenance man?' Sarah asked.

'He was wearing overalls and I'd seen him working around the building before.'

'What did you do then?'

'I managed to pull away from the doctor's grip. I ran out of the building as fast as I could.'

'Was there anything else you remember about the doctor,' Sarah asked.

Nancy hesitated. 'There was one thing...but I'm not sure.'

Sarah continued the questioning. 'Nancy, we're not here to judge you. It doesn't matter how small you think it is, it could still be useful.'

Sarah had done enough interviews to know that it was normal for anyone to be nervous. She knew it was important for Nancy to feel safe to talk.

'Well, I saw something.'

Sarah turned the page in her notebook. 'What do you think you saw?'

'I thought...he was holding something in his right hand.'

'What do you think it was?' Sarah asked.

'It looked like a knife. I left the basement in a panic. He used to tell me in my sessions that I was delusional so I'm not sure.

Sometimes I think he's following me but when I turn around...
there's no one there.'

Sarah leaned forward. 'Why did you drop the charges?'

Nancy hesitated. 'He terrified me. The day before the court
case, he rang and said that if I went to court, I would look like
a fool. People would laugh at me. I was always embarrassed,
and I hated myself. I was the weird kid at school and he knew
I covered my scars. He said the jury will know I'm crazy when
they see my cuts.'

James said, 'School can be horrible. It's a time when you can
feel the most self-conscious and embarrassed.'

'Yeah. It was pretty shit.'

'Did he say anything else?' James asked.

'He laughed and said, "Who's going to believe a neurotic
with a factitious disorder?"'

'Did you tell anyone that he called?' James asked.

'No. My head went crazy. I couldn't do it anymore.'

James voice softened. 'What do you mean you couldn't do
it anymore?'

'After his call I swallowed a heap of pills and ended up in
hospital. I can't remember calling an ambulance. I knew that
no one would believe me after that. My memory can be bad,
but I remembered everything he said. When he called, I could
hear evil. His voice was scary, and I couldn't stop shaking. Am
I crazy? Do you think you can hear evil?'

'If you are being threatened then it's understandable why
you could hear evil,' James responded.

Nancy's tears blurred her vision.

'Can I get you something, maybe a glass of water?' Sarah
asked.

'No thanks, I'm ok.'

James opened a file. 'I'm curious – who diagnosed you with
this factitious disorder?'

'He did. He said I had a compulsion to lie. I told him how I'd lied to police about wanting to kill myself. I didn't mean to lie. My parents were druggies and didn't care if I was dead. Child Services kept moving me to different foster homes. I felt like the world had dumped me. People cared if I said I wanted to kill myself. It felt good.'

'Are you getting any support now?' James asked.

'I have a really kind counselor at my church. She helped me to find a part-time job at Walmart. She said I'm smart and kind. No-one has ever said that to me before.'

'She sounds really supportive,' said James.

'Yeah she is. I don't watch the bad stuff on the news and I go for walks when my thoughts are busy. I also fundraise at the church.'

'That's great it's working out for you Nancy. I can hear you're working really hard to help yourself,' said Sarah.

'Some days aren't good, but I don't want to feel bad anymore.'

'We will need you to come down to the precinct for a formal statement. James and I can take you now.'

'Can I go this afternoon?'

'Sure. I'll arrange a police officer to pick you up at 2.00 pm. Does that suit?'

'Yes, that should be ok.'

'Are you sure that's ok? You sound a little hesitant,' said Sarah.

'Can I have a female cop pick me up?'

'Absolutely, Sarah responded. I'll arrange that for you. We'll see you at the precinct this afternoon. Thank you, Nancy. We appreciate your time. We know this hasn't been easy for you.'

As they left, Nancy looked up at the sky and thanked the world for her good feelings. She didn't feel lonely today. She felt they cared. She reflected on Sarah's kind words and enjoyed the moment. The noise in her head quietened. Nancy looked affectionately at Emmy brushing against her legs. 'I can see you're feeling good today too.'

SIXTEEN

GHOST WHISPERS

Two days had passed since Nancy provided her statement. Sarah had been a cop long enough to know Nancy was telling the truth. She wondered why he had taken her to the basement garage. Did he kill his clients there and put them in his trunk? Was there a place in the basement he stored bodies, or did his colleague wait in the basement and act as his accessory?

Sarah needed to get onto the killer's trail fast if they were going to find Curtis alive. She wondered whether more victims were being groomed.

They had held back long enough and now it was time to check out the basement. It was a risk that the psychologist might take off, but she hoped his arrogance at having outsmarted the police so far would keep him from running. She wanted to find out whether the psychiatrist Dr Cameron was involved, but he had been away on a conference, so they hadn't yet been able to talk with him. She couldn't think of anything more dangerous than two killers working together.

Despite giving James short notice to meet on Madison, he was there within thirty minutes.

They stepped into the elevator from the foyer. It rattled to the basement and gave a loud clunk as it stopped. Sarah imagined what it would have been like for his victims. Their terror would have begun here. Would they have felt any pain, or had they been anaesthetized? What would their thoughts have been about their trusted therapist turned killer? Had they frozen with fear or tried to run?

As the doors opened, Sarah shivered. 'Is this basement creepy or what?' Sarah asked.

'It's bloody creepy. Maybe there are ghosts telling us something.'

'Thanks James, I really needed to hear that. I'm spooked enough.' Then she whispered, 'Did you hear that?'

'Hear what?' James asked.

'I thought I heard voices. This place is getting to me.'

Sarah didn't know whether to believe in ghosts or not. Stories of ghostly sightings sometimes sounded genuine, but she was a facts and evidence person and found it difficult to get her head around anything supernatural. Her job was a constant reminder that people in the land of the living were the dangerous ones.

James noticed the walls were patterned with bird shit and water zigzagged across the concrete floor. It reminded him of the Catacombs of Paris. The difference was, this place wasn't a tourist attraction, and the guests were on a murder list.

'It would make sense why the psych was disturbed by a maintenance worker when Nancy was with him. This basement has serious water problems,' James said, tiptoeing across the floor.

'Tell me about it. It's a shocker. If anyone wanted to commit a crime, this would be the perfect place.'

'Why aren't there CCTV cameras down here? The security in this building is slack,' James said. As he approached the dumpster in the corner, he noticed something.

'Sarah, does this look like blood to you?'

'Mmm, maybe.'

When he took a closer look, he spotted a shiny object. Using his handkerchief, he carefully picked it up.

'Look what we have here. This is part of a cell phone. I wonder who owns this.'

Sarah stepped back. 'I think it's time we brought our team in to cordon off the area before we contaminate a crime scene. In the meantime, how about we pay our friend the psychologist a visit. I'm not sure you being a criminal psychologist will go down well with the doctor. How do you feel about walking into his office as a dumb-ass cop instead?' Sarah laughed.

'Good thinking. I'm a natural at that. I can also put on some dumb-ass accent if you like?'

'You're a great actor, James. I'm looking forward to it. Let's go rattle his cage.'

SEVENTEEN

DANGEROUS FAÇADE

The doctor's reception area was a noticeable contrast to the basement.

James studied the décor to help understand the doctor's personality. There was nothing out of place. A drink dispenser stood in the corner of the waiting room and three rows of magazines were displayed in order of subject matter across the coffee table. James wondered whether he was a psychopathic perfectionist.

Amateur artworks with cheap frames decorated the walls. *This guy didn't come from a wealthy family,* he thought.

Sarah tapped the desk bell. It wasn't long before an office door opened.

The doctor appeared unperturbed. 'Yes, can I help you?'

'We'd like to speak with Dr Ellison?' Sarah said.

'Yes, I'm Doctor Ellison.'

'I'm Lieutenant Wilkins and this is my colleague James Christianson. We're from the New York Police Department and we'd like to ask you a few questions. Is there somewhere private we can talk?'

Sarah knew she could be interviewing a serial killer. She maintained a composed demeanor.

'Certainly. We can use my office if you like. I have a client arriving soon, so I can't be too long.'

'That's fine,' Sarah said.

James followed Sarah, holding a pen and notebook. His eyes discreetly surveyed the office and the doctor. He noticed there were no family photos. Nothing that connected him to the outside world. A set of coloring-in books with a miniature Buddha sat on the doctor's shelf.

An imitation Shiraz rug lay under the coffee table. This reinforced the fact the doctor seemed to come from a working-class family. If he'd been deprived financially in his formative years, the effect of money could be intoxicating, James thought.

Sarah said, 'Doctor Ellison, I will get to the point. Sandra Lee was found dead in a Brooklyn alleyway and Brandy Johnson is in the city morgue. Both are clients of yours. We also have Courtney Williams and Janis Lang on our database as missing. Is it normal for your clients to end up dead or missing, Doctor?'

'I take on clients that other therapists won't touch due to their unstable patterns of behavior,' he replied smoothly, as he stroked his hair away from his forehead. 'Some of my clients have a history of sexual and physical abuse. It's not unusual for these clients to adopt maladaptive coping strategies which includes drug and alcohol usage. These precipitating and perpetuating factors can place them as high-lethality suicide attempters. Does that answer your question, Lieutenant?'

James carefully studied his body language. He was sitting up straight with his hands clasped in his lap. There was nothing to indicate he was lying. James wondered whether this control was learned or innate. The one thing he did notice was his hand-tailored suit. It would be worth more than anything in the room. His suit provided an insight into his financial situation.

'Do ya remember a former client of yours, a Nancy Fisher?' questioned James.

'Yes, I do. She made a complaint, which of course is not unusual for mentally disturbed clients.'

'She said ya called her a day before the court case. Is that correct?'

The doctor was quick to respond. 'The only call I made to Nancy was to check that she was safe. I was concerned that she was at risk of killing herself. She had no contact with family and friends so protective factors were limited. I'm sure you are aware of the duty of care responsibilities of a psychologist.'

'Why do ya think she made an official complaint about ya,' James asked.

'Clients like Nancy can be unsafe but also experience displaced feelings of frustration which they can project onto their therapists. Depressed clients can also experience short-term memory deficits which means their encoding and recall of information can be severely impaired. Nancy was depressed and has a factitious disorder, so I'm not surprised by her accusations. You see officer, she was extremely unwell and because of her vulnerability, she needed my support.'

James wondered how long he had rehearsed his academic speech. He knew the doctor's role-playing of authenticity and empathy would enable him to manipulate a client and gain their trust. He also knew that a depressed client taking the witness stand could be fatal to the case if the victim presented confused.

'I do apologize, but my client will be here soon. I need to prepare for my session. If I think of anything of importance I will let you know.'

'Before we go,' James said. 'Just thought you'd be interested to know...we've got our forensic team down in the basement garage.'

'Can I ask why you're interested in the basement?' Instead of responding to James, the doctor looked at Sarah.

She felt as if he was dissecting her. However, she reminded herself that he couldn't read minds.

'We are following procedures, Doctor,' Sarah replied. 'When there is a suicide, or we have a missing person, it is standard procedure to bring in our forensic team to the place of interest. I'm sure, being a Doctor, you understand we cannot make any assumptions. We need to assess all the relevant facts and evidence.'

Sarah didn't have to be a psychologist to know about internalized anger. She wanted to grab him by the collar and force him to tell her where Curtis was. She stepped towards the door before her emotions took over.

'Thanks for your time, Doctor. We will be in touch if there are any further questions.' As they moved out of earshot, she swore under her breath, 'We'll get you, you twisted bastard.'

James and Sarah were careful not to make eye contact until they were in the elevator and the doors were closed.

'What do you think?' James asked.

'I'm not sure what accent you were trying out there James, but you didn't sound too intelligent. It was perfect. Let him think we are dumb-ass cops. If he thinks he's smarter than us then he might get sloppy and stay put until we have enough evidence.'

James said, 'He sounded cold and creepy. My gut feeling is telling me he's bad. A Doctor Jekyll and Mr Hyde. Helper one day, killer the next.'

'Is there anything else you noticed?' Sarah asked.

'His office gives a snapshot of his past as well as his present. He has an imitation Persian rug and the paintings on the wall are amateurish, yet he wears a hand-tailored suit. I'm betting he comes from a working-class background and now he has a taste for the finer things in life. I wonder how he can afford an office on Madison.'

'Maybe he's an amazing psychologist and he's fully booked,' Sarah replied.

'Maybe you're right but operating in a prime location in New York, a sizeable chunk of your earnings goes on leasing. I also noticed he wasn't wearing glasses and I couldn't see any in his office. The glasses found next to the commissioner's niece could have been left by an accomplice.'

'What about lying? Did you notice anything?' Sarah asked.

'Nothing. If he's a psychopath, he won't exhibit a physical guilt response when he lies because he has no guilt. I had a sense that he was enjoying the moment. Laughing at us under his breath whilst he selectively suppressed and exposed information. There was one thing I noticed. He had a therapy coloring-in book on his shelf like the coloring-in book we found on Janis's coffee table. Unfortunately, even if her book has his fingerprints, it doesn't prove he has anything to do with her disappearance. It's not a crime to give clients therapy tools. Therapy tools or grooming tools, that is the question.'

'Christ. He's getting creepier by the minute,' Sarah stated. 'His colleague, Dr Cameron has been away for the last two weeks at a conference and he'll be back tomorrow. He has a tight alibi, but it doesn't mean we can cross him off the list. It will be interesting to hear what he's got to say. Let's see how the team is going in the basement.'

As they entered the basement garage, they noticed a police control vehicle blocking the entrance.

'You have a great team, Sarah. They've already cordoned off the area.' James meant what he said. He had witnessed enough crime scenes to know a professional one from a sloppy one. Sloppy work meant evidence being thrown out of court. It was a cop's worst nightmare if forensic photos or other evidence was inadmissible and months of an investigation went down the drain, especially if journalists had gained entry to a crime scene and contaminated crucial evidence.

'Found anything yet?' Sarah asked one of her team.

'We have some blood samples.'

'Great, call me if anything else comes up.'

Sarah knew blood samples could solve the case. It could lead to the killer. It was good news but it still didn't stop her worrying about Curtis.

EIGHTEEN

PICNIC IN THE PARK

I woke up feeling dizzy as hell in the back of a van. My head was throbbing where I'd been pistol-whipped. I wasn't sure whether it was sweat or blood running down my face. From what I could hear, there was one man driving and a passenger. My wrists and ankles were bound by zip ties and my head was covered with a hood.

I felt the pressure of my knife strapped to my leg. By pure luck, they had missed it. I clenched my teeth and desperately reached for the handle. It was then that the van came to a sudden halt. I was devastated. It was too late.

The back doors swung open. The best I could do was play dead. Hands gripped my ankles as they pulled me from the van. I wanted to scream with pain as I landed heavily on rough stones.

The sound of a dog barking broke the silence.

'Will you shut that fuckin' dog up!' a gruff voice yelled.

'It's only a duh...duh...dog. Ca...ca...can I...?'

'Do as you're fuckin' told or I'll put a bullet down your throat, you retard!'

I heard footsteps walking away then a gunshot followed by a high-pitched yelp.

The voice returned. 'He's fi...fi...finished. I du...du...dumped him in the barn.'

There was a stutterer and a dictator. The dictator took off my hood. 'We can toss this piece of shit in the barn. Let's eat before we do the dig and then we can bury him with that fuckin' dog. We'll kill two birds with one stone.' The dictator laughed.

His voice was chilling. *They've brought a packed lunch as if they're on a fuckin' murder picnic*, I thought. This was just another job for them. I wondered how many other bodies were buried in their killing field. *What the fuck am I going to do?* I was screwed.

'Fuckin' help me here. This guy's a dead weight.'

As they dragged my body to the barn, my head bounced up and down like a ball across a playing field. I kept my eyes closed and faked a gurgle, as if in my dying throes. I heard the unlocking of doors and felt the excruciating pain of being dragged again.

The sole of a boot pressed against my chest as if the killer was taking a rest. 'Great, he's choking on his own blood. Shit happens, my friend. Don't worry about giving a speech, someone can do that at your funeral,' he sneered.

'Where's the fuckin' dog? You said you dumped him in the barn.'

'He's under th...th...that tarp. I don't want rats eating him before we bury him. It will m...m...make m...m...me puke my lunch.'

I heard a set of doors slam shut but the sound of their voices was close by. Blood oozed from my mouth as broken teeth rolled around on my tongue. I remained still until the sound of their footsteps faded.

I spat out the teeth and opened my eyes. The wooden barn looked about a hundred years old and creaked with age. I noticed a dog peeping out from under a canvas tarp. The stutterer had lied. He hadn't killed the dog.

It was a black and tan German Shepherd and it belly-crawled towards me. He was emaciated and looked like a bag of bones.

I noticed blood coming from his hind leg and a rope was tightened around his neck.

'Jesus, buddy. How long have you had this rope around your neck?' *What is it about fuckin' dogs?* I thought. Now in the middle of nowhere I had a dog with sunken eyes and a tail that looked like a stick wanting my help.

I could feel the warmth of his injured body resting against mine as he licked my hand.

'We're in deep shit, buddy.'

I was drifting in and out of consciousness and badly wanted to close my eyes and escape the pain. I was sweating profusely. I felt like an animal ready for the slaughter. I realized I wasn't alone. I could see the shape of a man, then I heard footsteps leave the barn.

Is this when I get my just desserts? Am I paying the price for being a shithead?

'*Get up, Carter! Get your ass up or this will be the death of you!*' yelled a familiar voice.

I opened my eyes to see my old drill sergeant. I hadn't seen her since my army days. I'd trained at Fort Jackson, South Carolina, when I was twenty, thinking that joining the military would give me enough money to get through college. The problem was, my drill sergeant kicked me out for disobedience during basic combat training. I'd fucked that opportunity up bad. Now I was in a barn hallucinating.

'*Remember the code of conduct!*' the sergeant yelled. She bent down in her army greens and yelled again. '*Repeat after me: "If I am captured, I will continue to resist by all means possible. I will make every effort to escape and to aid others to escape!" Say it Carter, say the fuckin' code!*'

I could barely make a sound and she wanted me to repeat a fuckin' military code. A female bellowing at me before I died. This was truly a nightmare.

'*Obey your drill sergeant, say the code!*'

'You're not going to tell me what to say and I'm taking no orders from a woman who doesn't belong on the front line, so piss off!' *This can't be real. I'm supposed to see a light and go to a better place. Instead, I've got a female screaming in my face and a dog that wants to be rescued.*

'Say it! Say it now!'

'If I say it, will you piss off and leave me alone?'

'I want to hear the code!'

'If I am captured, I will...I will continue to resist by...all means possible...'

'Finish it off Carter! You're not dead, fuckin' finish the code!'

'I will make every effort...to escape...and aid others...to escape.'

Buddy wasn't moving, and blood was trickling from his wounds. The sergeant must be a final kick up the ass before I died.

'Now get your ass off the floor. Remember the drill – survival, evasion, resistance, and escape. Move your ass! Resist, resist, resist! Escape, escape, escape! Never leave your comrade! You know the drill!'

I couldn't believe it. I was almost dead, and my comrade was a dog. I hated dogs and I hated my sergeant.

'Move your ass off that floor. Get your fuckin' hands on that knife.'

With both hands bound, I reached for the knife. The barn was humid, and flies were circling. I gripped the knife's handle and with one yank, freed it from the strap on my leg. It took several painful maneuvers until I could cut the zip ties from my ankles and wrists.

Despite the dog's pain, he raised his head. The rope was embedded in the flesh around his neck. He didn't make a sound. His spirit was broken but his eyes were trusting. I saw the exposed raw flesh. Flies were buzzing around his malodorous wound and maggots weaved in and out. I scraped my knife gently across his skin to clear some of the maggots, wondering how long he had to live.

The sergeant continued to scream. '*Move, move, move! There's a crate. Get it now and move it to that window.*' She pointed to a small crate that looked as if it would collapse in a second. I could see a timber window at the far end of the barn.

'*The crate will give you the height to get through the window. Don't just fuckin' lie there. Move Carter! Move and get the crate!*'

NINETEEN

COMRADE

I crawled across the barn floor and peered through a gap in the timber wall. The dictator and the stutterer were leaning against a forest pine shoveling down lunch. They seemed no more than thirty feet away.

These guys are hungry. I might have enough time to get out of this hellhole.

The sergeant continued bellowing orders. *'Escape, survive, escape! Move, move, move!'*

I pulled the crate over to the back window of the barn.

'Climbing position, climbing position. You know the drill. Move your fuckin' ass! Move your ass. Move, move, move!'

Was this what they called post-traumatic stress? Was the army training so grueling that I was experiencing flashbacks or survivor's guilt?

I stepped onto the crate. I reached up to the window and pushed on the glass with both hands. As it swung open, parts of the frame crumbled. I knew that getting through the narrow opening was going to hurt.

I wondered whether Buddy could see the drill sergeant too. I had nothing to lose. It was time to escape.

I hoisted Buddy up so his torso was resting on my shoulder and his head was facing forward. I gently stepped back onto the crate. It wobbled precariously. I leaned towards the opening of the window, hoping Buddy would use my shoulder as leverage to push off so he could make it through with his injured leg.

'*Encourage and praise him. Do not yell at your comrade.*'

'Come on boy, you have to jump. Come on now.'

Within seconds, he let out a whimper and pushed forward.

I was waiting to hear him fall. *Will they hear us? Will they come running to check? Are we too late?*

'*Keep breathing. Keep breathing. Survive, evade, resist, and escape! Move your ass, Carter! It's your turn, move, move! You know the climbing drill. Use your strongest leg to push off and pull yourself up.*'

I gripped the knife between my teeth and pulled myself up halfway through the window. My skin shredded along the frame as if I was rubbing against a cheese grater.

'*Get into your falling position, Carter! Think of the forward roll. Focus, focus. Fall and roll, fall and roll! Protect your head and your back!*'

I did the fall and the roll was punishing. It was more like a heavy drop. Buddy was waiting. He had survived.

The sergeant leaned forward. '*In the crawling position! In the crawling position! Head down and to one side! Move your lazy ass, move! The dog will follow you. Move, move!*'

I remembered the military crawl as if it was yesterday. This was going to be a muscle-busting maneuver.

The sergeant screamed again. '*Push your body forward! Keep your head to one side, you know the drill. Crawl, crawl, keep down!*'

I wondered how I was going to escape with my body on fire. Every movement was a killer.

I pushed myself forward until I was in the undergrowth.

'*You're out of sight now! Stand up, stand up! Get ready to help your comrade!*'

I gripped onto a tree trunk for balance and turned sideways to see Buddy crawling with his head down. It was then

I realized Buddy was a military dog. I wondered how he had ended up in this hellhole.

'*Help your comrade, Carter. Squat down and place your comrade across your shoulders. Remember, give him praise.*'

'Good boy. You made it.' I knelt and ducked my head under Buddy's torso. I placed his bony body around my neck until his weary frame rested across my shoulders. Blood was spotting the forest floor. I wasn't sure if it was Buddy's or mine.

'*Move, fuckin' move! They'll follow the blood. You have no time!*'

I pushed my way through the prickly thicket and coarse undergrowth. This place had no walking paths. There wasn't a diner or public restroom waiting for me. This was private property, a haven for every plant species and creature. As I carried Buddy across my shoulders, I hoped I wouldn't step on a snake.

'*Keep moving, keep moving!*' the sergeant yelled.

I knew that it would be easy for them to track me. Did they deliberately leave me in the barn knowing I would escape? Was this their killing mountain and I'm their game? A killing range where they got their kicks out of the hunt.

'*Stop your thoughts and focus! Move your ass, they'll soon be on your trail. This is not a drill! I repeat, this is not a drill!*'

I could hear distant gunshots. I imagined the dictator's rage as he stood in the empty barn.

Buddy whimpered. He seemed lifeless but still recognized the sound of danger.

'*Move, move, and keep your comrade balanced.*'

The Fort Jackson drills had been grueling and now I knew why. I was done if I didn't keep moving. My body screamed with pain. I had to keep going. I was sure a rib was broken. I retched sporadically. Sliding down an embankment, I kept my grip on Buddy. He was so light it was easy to forget he was on my shoulders.

The undergrowth clawed at my skin but helped keep me upright. Memories of skylarking at an army camp stabbed at my conscience. I wondered how I'd thought the army was a joke.

'*Don't fuckin' stop or you're dead! Keep going! Move, move, move! At all costs, you must help your comrade. Focus, focus on your comrade. He needs your help!*'

I was desperate to rest. My legs wobbled. The ground was wet and my arms were aching.

I could hear gushing water.

'*Push forward! Push forward! Keep going or you'll be dead!*' the sergeant barked.

I realized the sergeant was right. It was life or death.

The ground was slippery. I knew if I twisted an ankle I was fucked and an easy hunt.

I made it to a creek, gazing at my only escape. The water gushed down a slope and looked more like a rapid than a gentle country creek.

The last time I was at a creek was when I was a kid fishing with my granddad. The water flowed gently, and we enjoyed a relaxing afternoon. My granddad used to listen to the football while I checked the lines. Now I was fighting for my life. As I stood on the bank, the blurred image of my granddad drifted in and out of sight. Had I just seen him, or was I going crazy? *Maybe I will wake up from this nightmare*, I thought.

As I strained to get a closer look, my granddad winked and pointed at a plank of wood.

I shivered. My hands trembled. The dog was still draped motionless across my shoulders. I didn't know how long I'd been standing still.

The sergeant's voice rang in my ears again. '*Focus, focus! Move! Keep going!*'

I stepped into the water, placing Buddy on the plank of wood. 'It's going to be ok, Buddy, you can do this.' I held on, hoping it would stay afloat.

In seconds, the current pulled us downstream. Suddenly, I was swallowing water and gulping for air. Water crashed around us. It was like a beast, beating us, whipping our bodies and pulling us along. Now I was fighting for my life with Mother Nature while being hammered by rocks.

I lost my grip on Buddy and saw him taken by the current. I managed to grab some reeds and hang on long enough to pull myself up on the opposite bank. I crawled out of the water on all fours to catch my breath.

'*You cannot abandon your comrade. Move, move, move! Keep going! Save your comrade at all costs! You know the code! Save your comrade now!*'

Jesus, I felt dead.

I turned around to see a glimpse of Buddy's head. He was being pushed further and further downstream. I leaned forward to regain balance. I had to move, or he would be gone. Who would have thought a creek in the middle of nowhere could be so fuckin' fierce?

The creek narrowed ahead as it swept around a corner. I saw a chance to grab Buddy. 'Please, someone, give me a break!'

I noticed an eagle gliding overhead. It turned its head to look down, watching my desperation. *I wish I had wings.*

I squatted on the rocks waiting for Buddy. If I slipped, we would both die in a watery grave. I could see the New York headlines: *Fisherman finds bodies of man and dog.*

'*Focus and stretch out your arms. Get into position! Get in position!*' the sergeant yelled.

Buddy looked like he was in a wash cycle. I lunged forward, grabbed his fur, and scooped up his fragile body. He looked up at me with unconditional trust.

'You're a trooper, you made it, Buddy.'

I cradled him in my arms and carefully stepped from one boulder to the next. It was then I noticed my wounded leg. I realized that adrenalin was numbing the pain.

I couldn't see the sergeant, but I could still hear her voice. '*Move, move, move! The enemy is on your trail!*'

TWENTY

BAD SEED

The man called Tony screamed in fury. Food and saliva sprayed from his mouth as he waddled from the barn. Broken blood vessels showed through his skin and his bulbous nose twitched with rage. He looked like a wild bull, ready to charge.

'You bloody idiot! He and that fuckin' dog have gone. You said you shot the dog.'

'I di...di...did, the bullet must have only g...g...grazed him.' Jonno was lying. He didn't have the heart to kill the dog.

* * *

Tony's fury commenced at birth. By the time he was five years old, he'd enjoyed drowning his family cat and setting alight his pet mice. His father used to laugh off his behavior and say, 'boys will be boys.'

At seventeen years of age, he lured his eight-year-old cousin into an upstairs bedroom during a family Christmas party by promising her candy. Once she entered the bedroom, he turned the lock. He casually walked over to his DVD player and turned the Christmas carols on high volume. No one heard her screams. No one heard her cries for help. When he had finished, he told her to get dressed and then threatened to kill her family if she mentioned a word to anyone. This was his first taste of power and he'd dreamed of the day he could keep his own girl chained in a cage to satisfy his lustful brutality.

Despite his cousin's terror, she found the courage to tell her mom. Her mom felt overwhelming guilt that she hadn't protected her daughter. She marched to her sister's home and knocked on the door. When her sister opened the door, she couldn't control her anger. 'Mary Jane says that Tony hurt her bad between the legs. He took her clothes off and said he would kill her family if she told anyone. I want to see Tony now! I want to ask him if this is true.'

Her sister screamed. 'My Tony would never hurt Mary! She's obviously lying. You're crazy! My Tony's a good Christian boy. He goes to church every Sunday. You've been drinking too much home brew. You know how liquor can mess with your head.' Her sister then slammed the door in her face.

She was enraged by her sister's response. She thought of their mom's words, 'be careful of those who protest too much, they're fighting the truth.' It was then she realized her sister was protecting her son.

Tony's parents were committed churchgoers and had given their son a wholesome Christian upbringing. They were suspicious of their son's behavior but couldn't bring themselves to admit their son would do such a thing.

His parents forbade him from playing with other children in the neighborhood because they considered them to be a bad influence on his morals. His hatred festered behind his Christian upbringing and he felt more and more isolated. During his pubescent years, he satisfied his sexual urges by lighting fires. He would sneak out at night and set alight anything that provided him with this ultimate primal pleasure. Watching the fury and destruction of the fires was sexually arousing. He rarely left the scene. If no one was around he'd hold his penis and pray to his God: 'Thank you God for giving me such plea-sures. Amen.' Little did his parents know his prayers in church were to a fire god. He was nearly caught several times while masturbating. He pretended to be rescuing animals.

When his parents discovered matches under his bed and smelt the smoke on his clothes, they took him to their priest for demonizing.

One night when his parents were asleep, he snuck into the family den. There he unlocked the gun cabinet and took out his father's pride and joy. It was a double-barrel hunting gun. A gun that had been handed down from his grandfather to his father. His father had taught him to hunt from the time he could walk. This night, he was going to hunt something different.

He smiled as he loaded the gun. At the base of the stairs, he glanced up at his parents' bedroom door. He tiptoed up the stairs in a heightened state of arousal, savoring every moment. Each step took him closer, each step gave him another dose of excitement.

The lounge room cuckoo clock chimed 2.00 am. He stood still. When the wooden bird retreated into its clock tower, he moved again. He smiled to himself. He believed he was special and this was his special mission.

He was going to destroy his memories of the days at church, his life of isolation, his life of praying with his family. He knew he would inherit everything. A house and the freedom to do whatever he wanted. It would be easy. There would be no struggle. There would be no one alive to contradict his story. This was the solution to his problem.

He gently opened the door to their bedroom. He stepped forward until he could feel the edge of his parents' bed against his leg. At point-blank range, he aimed the barrel at his mom's head. As he pulled the trigger, his father wakened to see his wife's head explode. He held up his hand and screamed. 'No! No! Please don't!'

'Don't worry...you won't feel a thing.'

He pulled the trigger again. His father's body shook with the force of the bullet. His eyes bulged with terror. Tony was thrilled. It was an easy job. He calmly rested the gun against the foot of the bed and dialed 911.

His police statement read: 'I have been beaten and raped for years. I killed them in self-defense. I was scared. They said they would kill me if I told anyone.'

The jury didn't buy his story and he was convicted of first-degree murder and sentenced to life in the penitentiary.

Although Tony was no longer a child, a human rights group stated it was unconstitutional that he was sentenced to life in prison as an adolescent and demanded his case be reviewed. They stated he had been an innocent victim of the most horrendous abuse and the immaturity of his adolescent brain, impaired his decision-making on the night he murdered his parents.

During this time, Tony had undertaken a Psychopathy Checklist and come out with flying colors. Portraying empathy for others was his forte so manipulating a questionnaire was a piece of cake.

With the killer's advocate group on his side, his high-test scores for empathy, his newfound love for God and his positive institutional behavior, he finally won over the parole board. The supreme manipulator was released after serving twenty-five years.

During Tony's time in the pen, he met plenty of sex predators and associated with some of the worst serial killers in New York State. It didn't take long to make useful connections with criminals on the outside. On his release, he started working for Mr X in New York.

His current assignment was to get rid of Curtis as quickly and cleanly as possible, but now things had fucked up. Now he was focused on a dumb-ass stutterer who couldn't do his job.

'You're an absolute fuckwit. When I asked you to check on him, what the fuck did you think I meant?'

'I...I...I did ch...ch...check on him,' Jonno stuttered. 'He was g...g...good as dead. No one has to know he g...g...g...got away, d...d...do they?'

'You fuckin' idiot! We tell Mr X we've completed our assignment and then the dead guy miraculously turns up? We're in deep shit, you fuckin' retard! Do you know how many clients we service? Once they find out we've lost this guy, we're the ones who're as good as dead! If the killers don't get us the cops will. America still executes retards like you. Don't think you'll get off the butcher's hook. We gotta get him.'

Jonno imagined killing the dictator but for now, he was careful not to enrage him further.

TWENTY-ONE

LETHAL DISPLACEMENT

Jonno followed Tony's orders while enjoying the fantasy of killing his tormenter. They walked behind the barn where they could see a trail of blood.

Tony rang Mr X. 'There's a small problem.'

'What do you mean, a small problem?' the doctor asked.

'Curtis's gone missing.'

'You mean he's got away?'

'Well, he hasn't exactly got away. He's taken off into the forest behind the cabin and he's headed for Esopus Creek. He's bleeding badly so he won't last long.'

'You better be right. I'll give you one hour and then I'm making a call. If you fuck this up, one of my men will blow your fuckin' head off, you got it?'

'Yessir! Don't worry, we'll get him.'

The doctor wasn't taking any chances. He called another of his thugs, a hitman who'd never failed him, and promised him a bonus to kill Curtis along with the two couriers.

Tony checked his handgun in its holster and grabbed his AK-47. He had assault knives, grenades, and homemade bombs, but the AK-47 with its telescopic sight was his baby. He hoped to spray enough bullets into Curtis to turn him into a million pieces. He also grabbed his ammunition pouch, which carried five fragmentation hand grenades. What he liked most about his grenades, was their lethal radius of sixteen feet.

Tony held out the grenade pouch to Jonno. 'Here, strap this to your waist. I'm going to blow him to bits if I get close enough.'

Jonno decided he wasn't going to be Tony's pack mule for grenades. He would wear the pouch for a short time. Carrying grenades terrified him. As he strapped the belt to his waist, he looked down nervously at the grenades sitting snugly in the pouch. He felt the urge to lie down as a wave of nausea swept over him. It was the same fear he'd experienced as a child walking home from school knowing his father was waiting. He gripped the machete for comfort.

'Why the fuck have you got a machete!' Tony screamed.

'We c...c...can clear the thick undergrowth. It's pretty b...b... bad out there.'

Tony grunted and loaded his AK-47.

On the ground, two drag marks were clearly visible.

Tony looked up at Jonno. 'The fuckin' dog's done an army crawl. You didn't adopt a military dog, did you?'

'You told me to g...g...g...get a vicious guard dog to protect the property.'

'You fuckin' retard. You got a dog trained for military combat. Now we have two escapees to kill. I want that dog's head in a bag. If we don't get them, you'll be fuckin' knee-capped, then try walkin' out of here.'

Jonno could only manage a nod. He looked at the long sharp blade of the machete, resisting the urge to hack into Tony's neck there and then. He walked ahead, cutting into the undergrowth.

* * *

Memories of Jonno's childhood resurfaced. His father had beaten the crap out of his mom. He could hear his father punch into his mom during a drunken rage. Jonno would curl up under his blankets, hearing her cries through his bedroom wall. He had struggled at school. He'd been severely bullied, and his speech impediment worsened with stress. His father would whip him in his drunken stupor and call him a stuttering dumb-ass. The beatings didn't stop there.

He was nine years old when he would hide in the closet trembling with fear until his father left for work. If his father found out he'd wet his bed, he wasn't allowed food for the day. There were times when his father's violent retributions left his butt raw with bloodied welts. To survive his childhood, he became submissive while fantasizing about the day he would kill his father.

During his early school years, he found the courage to tell his teacher why he couldn't sit down, a teacher he thought he could trust. He remembered the horror on her face as he told his story of the beatings.

She pulled him aside out of earshot of the other children. *At last,* he thought, *someone is going to listen to me. At last, someone is going to care enough to help me.* His teacher knelt down and whispered forcefully in his ear, 'That is a terrible thing to say about your daddy. I know your daddy and he is a God-fearing man. Don't you go telling lies, Johnathan Brown.'

Little did he know his father and his teacher had been fuckin' in the school gym since he'd started school.

That night, his father was waiting at the door. He got the worst beating of his life. His legs buckled with pain. It was the last time he trusted anyone. The last time he told the truth. He spent the rest of his adolescent years alone. The years of abuse stripped his self-worth. The days rolled into a feeling of nothingness. He wished the ground could swallow him and he would never have to face the world again.

Whenever he heard of a woman being tracked down and killed by her husband it terrified him. His mom had learned to stay. She'd learned to adapt. Running away was a death sentence.

When he turned fifteen, he grabbed his few possessions and escaped. He slept under a local bridge while sneaking back home to grab food on the days his parents worked.

He badly wanted to see his mom. He wanted to smell her perfume and feel her arms holding him. He was sure she knew he was sneaking into the house. There was always a meal wrapped in plastic with his favorite snacks. He wanted to leave her a note, but it was too risky. He fantasized about the day he would stand up to his father and reverse his brutality with a kitchen knife.

It didn't take him long to latch onto a criminal gang for survival. He eventually got busted when he was seventeen and was tried as an adult. Johnathan didn't know the law. He had no idea of mandatory sentencing until he faced the court. Without a character testimony, he knew he didn't stand a chance. The jury wanted him off the streets. He was convicted of robbery in the first degree and received a mandatory fifteen-year sentence.

The jury didn't want to know about his family background, they were tired of the victim stories and sick of the ever-increasing crime rate. Their minds and their hearts were closed.

The penitentiary became his family. He didn't belong to the outside world. It was during this time his father killed his mom.

When he was released, he felt lost. Thinking for himself was scary. Everything in the pen had been done for him. He couldn't understand the new technology. Getting onto a bus or train was frightening. He couldn't cope with people looking at him as if he was a dumb-ass. He felt like a child again. He knew there was no hope of getting a job. No one was going to employ an ex-con who couldn't read, had a stutter, and was scared of technology. The pen was the only life he knew.

While doing time, he'd met Tony. On Tony's last day in the pen, he gave him a Bible and said, 'When you get out, Johnny boy, don't forget to look me up. There's a contact number on page 666. I've already got some jobs lined up and you can work with me. No one gives a fuck about you on the outside. Remember, once a crim always a crim. People are gonna judge you wherever you go but don't worry, I'll look after you.'

It didn't take him long until he'd pulled out Tony's Bible and called the number. Tony set him up with accommodation and gave him work. He'd worked for Tony for several years but now he'd had enough. He rarely got paid, he lived in shit accommodation infested with bugs, and worst of all, he was constantly called a dumb-ass. He felt trapped and his internalized memories of his father resurfaced.

* * *

Tony knelt to inspect the water's edge. 'The son of a bitch crossed the creek and the dog's still with him. You go across first, I'll follow.'

Jonno knew he wasn't going to cross the creek with a grenade pouch strapped to his waist. For one thing, he couldn't swim and for another he didn't want to be blown to bits underwater. He looked submissively at Tony just as he had done a hundred times before.

Tony leaned down and placed his hand on a piece of driftwood. 'You can lie on this. It's the perfect float for you. Are you listening, you fuckin' dumb-ass?'

Jonno felt perspiration trickle down his face. His body trembled. His thoughts flashed back. He saw his father raise his belt. He felt the same fear. He felt warm piss run down his legs. He saw his father's drunken eyes and heard his slurred commands: 'You fuckin' good-for-nothing piece of shit. This is the last time you talk to your teacher.'

Unable to suppress his rage any longer, he raised the machete and swung the blade down on Tony's wrist with precision.

Blood sprayed across Tony's face as his hand fell onto the creek bank. He screamed in horror and pain.

When he turned to look up at Jonno, he saw the machete in motion again. Tony fell backwards as the blade sliced once more. His neck was now a gaping hole. Jonno could see his father beating his mom. He was enjoying every slash of his weapon. He swung it over and over. He wiped the blood off his mouth and smiled with cathartic exhilaration.

'No one f...f...fucks with me anymore. No one tells me w...w... what to fuckin' do and calls me a dumb-ass!' he screamed.

It was over. He now had the power. He was proud of himself. Tony hadn't suspected a thing. He pushed the torso into the creek and watched it disappear downstream.

As Jonno bent down to wash the blood from his arms he suddenly froze. He could hear something. Someone was present. A tall figure was reflected in the water. The shadow leaned over and he felt cold metal pressed against his neck.

'Where's Curtis? Tell me now or you're a dead man.'

'He's d...d...dead. I shot him and d...d...d dumped him in the creek.' He sensed the killer was not convinced.

Jonno gazed at the sunlight reflecting off the water's edge. It was going to be his last vision of the world. His eyes welled with tears. He looked up to the sky and prayed for forgiveness from his mom. *I'm sorry I couldn't protect you.* It was then he smelt her perfume and heard her gentle words. 'It's ok, Johnathan. You deserved safety and I'm sorry I didn't give you that. You're leaving this world but don't be afraid, I'll be with you.'

Johnathan closed his eyes. He felt the sweetest peace.

His life was extinguished as the trigger was pulled.

The tall figure called his boss. 'Curtis got away across the Esopus Creek and he's headed for Interstate 87. Don't worry, we'll be waiting for him at the other end.'

'Call me when he's dead. You'll get a bonus when I know his blood is on the interstate.'

TWENTY-TWO

PRIDE

As I moved from the creek's edge, I heard the echo of gunshots. Buddy whimpered, and birds took flight from nearby trees. It didn't make sense. Who was firing a gun? If it was the police, there would surely be a chopper overhead.

I guessed it wasn't the police. Oh man, I was in deep shit. If I could find a road, I would have a chance of escaping. As I turned back and looked at the creek, I saw what looked like body parts. *Was my mind playing tricks?*

'Sorry Buddy, stay here, I'll be back.'

I ran back to the creek's edge and saw a body moving towards me, bobbing up and down in the current. I spotted a gun holster strapped to the torso.

My shoulders burned with the force of the water as I grabbed the body and held it long enough to unclip the holster strap. Now I could see the handgun. Now I knew I had a chance of getting back to New York. I strapped the holster to my waist and carried Buddy. I wasn't going to let those bastards get us now.

I noticed the eagle again. Hovering above, he looked down as if acknowledging my displacement in his world. The humidity was stifling, and perspiration stung my eyes. In one majestic swoop, the eagle glided past. I wondered what it could see that I couldn't.

My feelings of helplessness were interrupted by my grand-mother's voice: *'Curtis, you have tunnel vision. Let go of your pride. Open your eyes and your mind.'*

I looked up again and followed the eagle's direction as it glided from the creek's edge. My head throbbed, and my body shook as if I'd received an electric shock. I staggered along with Buddy still on my shoulders until I heard muffled voices coming from a small clearing.

I gently placed my comrade on the forest floor and crawled closer to the voices. Stones stabbed at my knees and hands. As I peeped through the clearing, I saw a couple and in the distance, a farmhouse.

I looked back at Buddy. 'Luck is on our side.'

I cradled him in my arms and approached the farmhouse. Someone yelled, 'Jesus, man! What the fuck happened to you?'

'I've got to get help for my comrade and I need to get to Brooklyn.'

'You need a doctor, you look like shit. And your dog needs a vet.'

'Please...don't take me to hospital. I'll be ok. I'll explain later.'

'Hey man, not while you've got that gun strapped to your waist. I'm not helping until you take that belt off.'

The man took several steps back with his hands in the air. I placed Buddy down and unclipped the belt and placed it gently on the ground.

The man looked at his wife.

'You don't need my permission, Cole. They need your help. Don't forget to text me once you get to a vet. I'll get a rug and some water for the trip.'

It was then my legs wobbled, and the world became blurred. The last thing I remember was the ground spinning as if I'd downed a bottle of bourbon in one gulp.

TWENTY-THREE

THE BROTHERHOOD

I awoke on the back seat of a pickup and shot up in fright. One moment I'm dreaming of Sarah and the next I was lying on a hard vinyl seat. *Where the hell am I?* I thought.

'Where's my comrade?'

'Hey man, it's ok. I've just dropped him off to the best vet in the county and it sounds like he's gonna pull through. I used a little persuasion though. I just picked the vet up by his coat collar and once his feet landed back on the ground, your dog became a priority. He's now top dog of that clinic.' He grinned and puffed on a cigarette.

I knew then, not to fuck with this guy.

'You still wanna get to Brooklyn?'

'Yeah. I've got to get there somehow.'

'I'm Cole,' he said. There was a considerable pause before he continued. 'My poppa would be proud of you. I'll help ya out for him. He'd want me to do that. He loved dogs. He would cut off a guy's balls who hurt a dog,' he laughed.

This guy had a crazy laugh.

'Do ya have a name?'

'It's Curtis.'

'Ok Curtis, what's going on with you and ya comrade?'

If I wanted this guy's help I had to tell him something. 'Just not sure who's after me. I was doing some undercover work and now I'm in deep shit.'

'Does that mean you're an undercover cop or something?'

'I'm not a cop but you're close.'

'Whoever you work for, do they know where you are?'

'Not yet. I can't go to hospital or I'll end up...a corpse.'

'Brooklyn, it is. I hope ya tellin' me the truth or I'll scalp ya and hang it from an interstate post.'

I noticed he didn't laugh. I guessed he would do exactly that.

It felt good to be on the road, but talking was exhausting. My head drooped, and I fell into a deep sleep. The next thing I knew I woke up to country music and Cole tapping his fingers on the wheel.

'You're finally awake; I was hoping you weren't in a coma. You really belong in a hospital bed. There's a water bottle in the back. You'd better have a swig before ya pass out again. You look like death warmed up. I'm stoppin' at this diner. You good for a burger?'

'Sure,' I said.

I wondered why he would trust me. Maybe he sensed I was the good guy. I also wondered how I was going to eat a burger with a mouth of broken teeth and feeling half dead.

As Cole pulled up in front of the diner, he gave me a phone number.

'Here's the vet's number for Buddy. You'll have to call them and let them know what to do with ya dog once he's patched up.'

'Thanks,' I responded.

Calling the vet was easy. Giving out Sarah's contact number was hard. I didn't want to burden Sarah but there was no one else I could trust to look after my comrade.

'You wait here. We don't want to scare the customers. And by the way, I've got ya gun. You'll get it back once I've dropped you off.'

* * *

As Cole walked towards the diner, the smell of eggs and bacon lifted his spirits. He opened the spring action door and saw a sea of black jackets, beards, tattoos, and piercings.

'Well, look what the cat dragged in. If it isn't our old buddy Cole. Where have ya been, you old fart?'

It was Big Red, the sergeant-at-arms and the rest of his brothers of the Black Taipans Motorcycle Club. Cole was amazed that Big Red hadn't changed. He had a curly red beard and a nose as wide as his face. Red had been kicked out of the army for his wild behavior as he wasn't suited to rules and regulations. He was a loose cannon and he liked drinking, women, guns, and he loved his mom. If anyone had anything bad to say about a woman or hurt a kid, they were mincemeat.

'What brings you here?' Red asked, giving Cole a slap on the back and a hug.

'I'm giving a guy a lift to New York. He's chillin' in my pickup.'

Red nodded and glanced at Cole's neck. 'You've only got a scar now but you're always welcome in our club.'

Cole had been a member for six years. The words 'Black Taipans' had been removed from Cole's neck by laser when he'd left the club. They'd escorted him to a clinic to remove the tattoo. He'd respected their rules. Although he'd felt sad to say goodbye to his 'family', the Black Taipans were a club you didn't fuck with. The last thing he would have done was piss them off. Cole missed his brothers. He missed the sound of the mean machines, the adrenalin rush with the freedom of a fast ride, and the sweet smell of tobacco.

Inside the diner, Cole recognized a comrade, Animal. He was devouring a burger and licking the juices running down his fingers. Animal had got his nickname from rescuing injured animals on the roads. He could shoot a man dead any day and enjoy the thrill, but shoot an animal? That was unthinkable. It irritated everyone, as he would hold up a bike run to drop off injured animals at the local vets. Every vet in New York knew him, and he never got a bill. There was an unspoken agreement. One look at his comrades waiting outside would make any vet amenable.

Like several other club members, Animal had had a tough life. Cole found this out when he'd joined the club. Animal was an only child and his father had abandoned their small family years before he was a teenager. In his teenage years, Animal's mom suffered severe depressive episodes and was addicted to crack. During this time, Animal was diagnosed with ADHD and prescribed dexi to help him sit still in class. Unfortunately, the family doctor was a pushover for handing out drugs and his mom regularly filled the prescriptions for her own use.

In her psychotic episodes, she would tell her son to fuck off and go hang himself. Although Animal hated her, it didn't stop his overwhelming feelings of rejection. One night in her drunken stupor, she overdosed on crack.

After his mom's death, he found the Taipans. The club became his family, a family that didn't reject him or judge him. Brothers who didn't care whether he could read or write. They didn't care that his mum was a crackhead and his dad was a loser. They took him under their wing and provided protection. The club gave him a purpose and a sense of belonging.

Animal gazed outside the diner window as images of his mom faded. Then something caught his eye. He noticed a guy in the parking lot clutching his side. He was staggering as if loaded with drugs and looking over his shoulder. Something wasn't right. He wondered why he was acting like a wanted man.

TWENTY-FOUR

COBWEBS

Motorcycles were lined up outside the diner. *Interesting customers*, I thought. I needed a piss and couldn't wait. I spotted an old restroom that looked like spider hotel.

I had a fear of spiders and imagined creepy crawlies on the restroom walls. I'd been bitten by a spider as a kid when I'd put on my trainers and been sick as a dog for days. At first, I'd thought it was a thorn until I saw the spider squashed against my sock. Since then, I'd always checked and rechecked any closed-in shoes.

As I approached the restroom, I nearly lost my balance. It was difficult to keep steady without looking like a drunk. I glanced around, hoping I wasn't being followed. My lips were dry and cracked and there was a stabbing pain in my side.

I took the quickest piss of my life while watching out for any miniscule movement or set of hairy legs ready to pounce on my shoulder. I'd heard of exposure therapy to help get over fears, but it just didn't make sense to be scared of something so small. I felt like a wuss and wasn't going to admit my fear to anyone.

Once I'd left the restroom I decided to check out the diner. I wasn't going to spend my time in the vehicle ruminating about Sarah. I needed a distraction. Once inside, I slumped into the closest booth.

'Hey man, what the hell happened to you?' asked a red bearded guy sitting with Cole.

I had an audience. At least thirty leather jackets were staring me down.

'Curtis, I'd like to introduce Big Red, the Black Taipan's sergeant-at-arms, and Animal, the road captain who organizes the best runs in New York.'

I gave a slight nod. The name Black Taipans seemed so fuckin' clichéd, I thought. Then again, who was I to talk? I was a clichéd loser. Their jackets were emblazoned with a picture of a snake with its head raised ready to strike. They looked as though they'd just walked off a 1970's movie set for a coffee break before the next shoot.

A voice zapped me back to reality.

'If you're a buddy of Cole's, you're a pal of ours,' Red announced.

Now I was a lost dog who had just been adopted. *Great,* I thought. *Life's looking up.*

My head begged for a pillow. I felt as if I'd been anaesthetized and had only seconds to stay awake. My head fell forward until my forehead was resting on the table.

'Hey, don't sleep yet. Wake up! Here's ya burger with the lot.'

I looked up and saw the cook wipe his sweaty face on his greasy apron.

'Good grub here,' Animal grunted.

I couldn't help but stare at a snake emblazoned on his jacket.

'You like the snake?' Animal asked.

'Mmm, pretty cool,' I said.

'It's a defender, it only attacks if someone attacks it first.'

There was a noticeable silence. Jesus, I hoped he wasn't warning me.

I noticed Animal was sharing his food with a rat. Its pink nose and whiskers peeked out of an opening in the top of his jacket. I couldn't help but see the irony of a snake and a rat together. *Maybe this guy has a soft side.*

'This is Rat and don't worry, he doesn't bite,' Animal laughed.

I thought of Charlie skittering around my apartment waiting for a meal.

And here I was. One day I'd been dreaming of buying a cruiser, the next I was sitting with the Black Taipans looking like fuckin' road-kill. To make matters worse, I was with a road captain and a sergeant-at-arms who looked like they could crush a skull with their bare hands.

I imagined what it would be like riding the roads, not giving a damn about anything but the club and the road ahead, wearing a club jacket and feeling free.

As a kid, I'd had a pal whose dad was a rev-head. On weekends, we went trail bike riding or tinkered with his dad's collection of motor engines. Bikes terrified my mom. She called them coffins on wheels.

I'd always read about motorcycle clubs being gangs. The irony of it all was that I felt safer with the Taipans than with the sharks on Wall Street. I could see them now, walking around in their fuckin' hotshot suits, living their piss-weak lives and driving sports cars, hoping that would enlarge their cocks. They were the assholes who stabbed you in the back and thought their shit didn't stink while they ripped off some poor unsuspecting retiree and snorted white powder on their breaks. Wall Street thugs in business suits.

The cook came back with a med kit. He soaked my wounds with antiseptic. The pain was excruciating, but I didn't flinch. I wasn't going to look like a city wuss in front of these guys. He wrapped up my wounds like a pro.

'Our chef's an expert with wounds. He's had plenty of practice, but it's been a while since he patched any of us up. You bring back happy memories, Curtis,' Animal grinned.

I hoped Animal was joking but watching the cook's skill with a bandage, I doubted it. I think they liked me. Maybe I looked like some tough guy who would die without a cause. Little did they know I would give anything to be watching the Chicago Cubs with a bucket of popcorn.

My thoughts drifted back to Sarah. I hoped she wouldn't ditch me for being an asshole.

TWENTY-FIVE

FBI

The boys stood up, ready to leave the diner.

Red looked at Cole. 'I miss our days shootin' the breeze.'

'Yeah, the world is spinnin' too fast. Now with the farm and the family, time doesn't stand still.'

They both sounded genuine. It was easy to see Cole was respected by the club.

'See ya man,' said Red, with a goodbye hug.

I'd never seen bikers hug each other and I still couldn't understand why Cole was going out of his way to help me. This guy had done more for me in one day than any friend had done in my entire life. *The world isn't full of douchebags after all,* I thought.

'We're still a fair distance from Brooklyn so ya better take this,' Cole said, passing me a soda and a Hershey bar. 'This will help you survive for a while. Now let's get on the road.'

Cole Chuckled. 'Jesus Curtis, you look like a fuckin' mummy headin' for a museum.'

'Yeah, well I feel like one.'

Cole pointed out a black Chrysler at the far end of the parking lot. 'Where did that come from? Why isn't anyone gettin' out?'

'Maybe they've stopped for a quick piss,' I responded.

'It's not lookin' good. Let's keep an eye on these guys. I'll bet ya they pull out the same time we do.'

He was right. Once out of the parking lot, we were followed.

Cole was on his cell to Red in seconds. 'Hey Red, we've got trouble here. A black Chrysler is right up our ass.'

'Don't worry Curtis. We have the Taipans as our backup. You're in good hands.'

Somehow, I wasn't convinced.

'There's a packet of ammo on the floor and here's a 12-gauge shotgun of mine and your handgun!'

The shotgun was easy to load. I knew shooting from a moving vehicle was going to be unpredictable. The drill sergeant leaned over the front seat. *This is up to you now. You know the drill. It's time to think for yourself.*

As the sergeant disappeared, I loaded the shotgun and steadied it into position. I gently rested the tip of its muzzle through a gap in the back window.

'Keep drivin' at the same speed. Look straight ahead!' I shouted to Cole.

The Chrysler crept closer. Keeping my head low, I readied the gun for firing. With my heart thumping, I took aim, praying I would hit the target. I had to breathe. *Focus, focus. Accuracy and precision are everything,* I reminded myself. The Chrysler continued to edge up until I could see the mudguard. The rear window came down in what seemed like slow motion. A semi-automatic was aimed at Cole. I fired several rounds until I heard the Chrysler screech away. It spun out of control and slammed into a tree. I hadn't expected it to be over so quickly.

'How did ya learn to shoot like that?' Cole yelled.

'From an absolute asshole of a drill sergeant.'

'Well that bad ass of a drill sergeant just saved your life.'

I noticed Cole kept his eye on the rear-vision mirror.

'We're not out of trouble yet, Curtis, we have more company. There's an ambulance approaching fast.' Cole sounded alarmed.

I was confused. An ambulance should be a relief.

'Jesus, Curtis, you have the FBI after you!' Cole yelled.

'The FBI driving an ambulance? I doubt it.'

'It's the FBI. Trust me, Curtis.'

'How the hell do you know?'

'The windows are tinted and bulletproof. It's an armored vehicle. They're designed for rammin'. The FBI aren't always the good guys, y'know. Sometimes they work for the bad guys.'

I reloaded the shotgun.

'I hope you're right, Cole. I don't want to be killing a fuckin' medic.'

At that moment, the ambulance came roaring up and past our vehicle. The back-double doors flew open.

Cole's pickup was showered with bullets. I knew the tires had been shot and I was waiting for the vehicle to flip. I tightened the belt strap across my chest and curled in a crash position ready to take the full impact.

The sound of crushing and twisting metal was deafening. Our pickup flipped several times down a small embankment and then came to rest upside down.

TWENTY-SIX

THE DEATH OF A BROTHER

The Taipans didn't take long to catch up. They had seen Cole and Curtis being forced off the road.

Red pulled his crowbar out of his tank bag while traveling close behind Animal. A crowbar was a handy tool, especially to scare the shit out of fuckwits who got their thrills driving bikers off the road.

Animal roared up behind the ambulance. The doors opened again. Before he had the chance to do anything, he saw an automatic. He looked back at his brothers. A burst of gunfire flashed. As the ambulance sped off, Animal's bike flipped through the air before crashing into a ditch.

The bike was a heap of scrap metal and Animal's mangled body lay several feet away. It was a sickening sight. Red skidded off the road. He rushed to Animal's side and the rest of the brothers gave up the pursuit. They were no match for an automatic. Red held Animal in his arms and rocked him like a baby.

'You're a bloody good brother, Animal.'

Animal felt safe. He was in the arms of a brother who loved him.

'I'm here for ya Animal. You're not lookin' good, but I forgive ya.'

Although Animal was coughing up blood he managed to grin.

Red reached into Animal's pocket and gently pulled out Rat. 'Your buddy survived. I'll make sure he gets the best treatment.' Red held Animal closer. 'Do ya remember the time we got drunk on the beach and decided to go swimmin? The surf was so rough it ripped off your swimmers. You laughed so hard you couldn't stand up.'

'Yeah,' Animal gasped as his breathing becoming increasingly labored. 'Happy memories,' he whispered, gripping Red's arm.

Animal's grip on his arm slowly loosened. Red continued to rock him back and forth in his arms until the light in Animal's eyes died. Red couldn't stop his tears.

* * *

The doctor received the call that made his blood boil. 'How hard is it to catch an idiot? I pay big money and I still can't get any fuckin' results! Get back on his trail. I want to know exactly where he is at all times.' The doctor canceled his appointments for the day and prepared his killing tools. *You're finished, Curtis,* he thought. *I'll take great pleasure in finishing you off, you loser.*

He would get to Curtis before he could spill the beans to the cops, and then, maybe, he'd think about moving away from New York.

TWENTY-SEVEN

NEW YORK

I opened my eyes and immediately smelt gas. There were no guns in sight. I crawled out of a mass of metal. I didn't have a scratch on me, but I was groggy.

'Cole, can you hear me! Cole, it's Curtis, are you ok?'

'Jesus, Curtis, you really know how to stuff up someone's life. Stop bashing my ears with that screamin'!'

Even with his life in danger, Cole had a sense of humor.

It took all my strength to support his head and drag him a safe distance away.

Just in time. The pickup exploded, and metal missiles flew overhead.

'Help is coming Cole, just keep still.'

'Well, I'm not goin' anywhere soon. Sorry Curtis, but I'm not in any shape to drive.'

'I'm the one who got you into this mess. I'll work it out. You have to get to a hospital.'

When the brothers arrived, something didn't look right.

Red approached me. Was I going to be whacked?

He placed my arm around his shoulders.

I sighed with relief.

'Do ya still need a ride?' Red asked.

'Yeah, but I can find my own way.'

'No one fucks with the Taipans. Whoever killed Animal and injured Cole aren't gonna get away with it. Whatever your mission is, I want ya to finish the job.'

'You mean a brother was killed?' I asked.

Red didn't answer.

As he helped me up the embankment, I knew there was no going back. I was going to get the monster of New York.

'I don't have a spare helmet, but do ya think you can stay on the bike?' Red asked.

'Yes,' I answered. I had to get to Brooklyn. There was no choice but to hang on tight.

'Climb on back then, Curtis. I want ya to get this fuckin' scumbag!'

'I have to call an ambulance for Cole and Animal?'

'The boys've already taken care of that. Here, you're gonna need this.'

Red handed me a Desert Eagle pistol. 'Here's some ammo as well. She's quite weighty but a beauty.' From Red's bike pack, he also took out a cell. 'I always keep a few handy. You never know when ya gonna need a spare. The number's on the back.'

TWENTY-EIGHT

GAS LIGHTING

Sean Young lived alone and had no contact with his family. It wasn't until he attended The Manhattan Well-being Clinic that his battle with cutting ceased, along with his disordered eating and sleeping patterns. His nightmares reduced, and he slept more than three hours a night.

He was seeing a psych who filled a void in his life. He no longer felt abandoned by the world. His psych was the only one who listened and validated his feelings. He couldn't believe how much he cared about his well-being. On his first appointment, he had been fearful that the psych would think he was a loser. Now he felt free to talk about anything without being judged.

Sean had been sexually abused by a family friend when he was eight years old. The abuse occurred several times until he'd told his mom. Her response was that it was his fault and he'd been a headache since the day he was born. She'd told him to man up and get over it. There were no charges laid against his rapist and the traumatic experience made him feel disconnected from his once safe world. Everyone seemed threatening.

Before he met his psych, he used to hear punishing voices that depleted his self-esteem. He would hear his mom's voice: *'You're always stuffing up, you imagine everything, I really wonder*

about you, I really don't know what you're going on about, you're
crazy. I should have aborted you when I had the chance.'

Her words were emotionally debilitating. He believed
he was crazy. The only time his mom had showed him any
affection was in front of others, manipulating the impression
of being a loving mother. She would say, *'I can't imagine why*
anyone wouldn't want to have children. People like that are so self-
ish. It's the most fulfilling thing anyone could experience. I love my
son so much I would run in front of a truck to save him.'

Because of his mom's on-going verbal abuse, he couldn't
remember a time when he'd had friends over, fearing she would
embarrass him. He'd thought he'd escaped his unhappiness
when he'd found a supportive girlfriend until he discovered
she'd been cheating. She'd been his confidant, best friend and
lover. The feeling of loss and loneliness had suffocated him.

Sean had always pushed down his feelings until one day at
seventeen, he could no longer take it and unleashed his anger,
erupting like a volcano. His mom told him he was a psycho and
kicked him out of home. It was a blessing in disguise. He found
supported accommodation, got a job, and was then able to rent
his own place. He began to have hope for the future. He could
make decisions without being criticized or undermined.

He still couldn't help but envy his friends who had loving
relationships with their parents. He wished he had a normal
family. Despite all his mom's abuse, he felt sorry for her and
hoped one day she would love him.

His psych diagnosed him with generalized anxiety,
post-traumatic stress disorder and depression. His psychological pain was relentless. Seeing his psych helped him cope with
his demons.

Spending his days in bed curled up in a fetal position was
now a thing of the past. He was determined to free himself
from his never-ending cycle of disempowerment. Although he
was still taking antidepressants he looked forward to a future

free from pills.

He found it difficult to talk about his past. His psych held the key to his dark secrets, helping him to develop coping skills. Most of all he helped him to like himself and to accept that he had special qualities. He learned to replace the critical inner voice of his past with positive self-statements.

He was meeting his psych in Central Park early today, at 5.30 am, and was excited to start what the doctor called cognitive environment therapy. He had convinced him that he still had a distorted view of the world and was seeing and hearing things that didn't exist, causing him to be imprisoned by rigid thoughts and non-existent dangers. His psych assured him that CET would be a positive step towards well-being and psychological healing, and that the therapy would soon be recognized worldwide and published in a psychological journal.

Sean knew he needed ongoing strategies to help himself and because he feared losing his psych's support, he was willing to try anything. He didn't want to ask too many questions about the therapy and appear stupid. He wanted to please his psych and keep hearing him say, *'I'm proud of you Sean. You're doing well.'*

He trusted his psych's personalized therapy. Seeing him gave his life meaning. At Christmas, his psych gave him a precious stone and said it signified courage. The gift made Sean feel special.

Some mornings, he felt weighed down, as if a concrete slab was on his chest, but this morning he sprang out of bed. He grabbed his backpack and earphones, and jumped on a bus to Central Park.

The bus arrived on time at 5th Avenue, a short walk away from their arranged meeting place. He was a perfectionist and time meant everything. He didn't want to be late today and risk a panic attack.

Making direct eye contact with people made him feel

vulnerable, so he walked with his head down. It didn't seem so long ago that he'd believed he was dead and was walking amongst the living. As it was early morning, there were very few people on the streets. He took a deep breath and changed his pace. *Is someone following me? Am I in danger? It's ok, I'm just imagining it,* he thought, challenging his self-defeating thoughts just like his psych had taught him. *I'm safe, I'm ok. I'm having an irrational thought.*

Sean stood at the intersection waiting for the lights to change. Across the intersection, he could see his psych. He frantically waved at him and breathed a deep sigh of relief.

When the lights changed, he stepped in the crosswalk, but a van pulled in front of him and blocked his view. He couldn't understand why a van would stop in a crosswalk. The side doors of the van opened and in a flash, he was pulled inside. The doors immediately closed with a bang and the van took off at speed. *Is this a cruel joke?* he thought. But he realized it wasn't a joke. He was living his worst nightmare. He hoped his psych had seen him and would call the police. Someone else was in the van. He felt zip ties being tightened around his ankles and wrists. The smell of a sickly cologne contributed to his nausea. Sean's body trembled as duct tape was pulled across his mouth and a hood was placed over his head. His world spiraled out of control as he lay in darkness.

This fear was real. He was not hallucinating. *I'm going to die, this is it,* he thought. He struggled to breathe. What were they going to do to him? Were they going to keep him prisoner or kill him and dump his body? He felt a familiar wetness and warmth.

'You bastard, you've pissed everywhere.'

Sean felt a sudden pain to his head. His stomach lurched and with it, a desperate need to vomit.

'Stop moving or I'll blow a hole in your fuckin' head. You got it?'

He felt something hard pressing against his cheek, possibly a gun. Sean sensed he was disposable. His life could be over in minutes.

'Now you be a good boy, you hear me?'

At the best of times, Sean over-analyzed and now his thoughts were racing at a million miles an hour. He hated himself for not being able to fight back. He hoped his death would be quick.

TWENTY-NINE

ONE STEP CLOSER

Sarah finally got the break she'd been hoping for. There was an eyewitness account of a pedestrian being pulled into a van on the intersection of 5th Avenue and East 78th Street. A hot dog vendor named George setting up for the day thought he had witnessed a possible abduction. Sarah hoped it was connected to the doctor. It was close to his office on Madison and opposite Central Park where he liked to do his so-called cognitive environment therapy.

James was already on the scene when Sarah arrived. He was glad the eyewitness was still there rather than at the precinct. Interviewing at the crime scene was better for eyewitness recall and consistent details.

Sarah noticed the witness was clearly shaken. 'Hi George, I believe you may have witnessed a crime?' she asked him.

'Yes, ma'am.'

'Tell me in your own words what happened.'

'Well, I was setting up my equipment, when I saw a young guy on my side of the street. He started walking in the cross-walk. A van came charging up the street and suddenly stopped, blocking him from crossing. It frightened the hell out of me. I thought he was going to get hit. A guy jumped out and pulled him into the van.'

'Could you describe the guy who was pulled into the van?'

'He was wearing jeans and a white top. He had blonde hair.'

'How old do you think he was?' Sarah questioned.

'He looked in his early twenties.'

'What about the man who pulled him into the van. Are you able to describe him?' Sarah asked.

'He was wearing a black hoodie. Sorry, it happened so quickly. That's all I can remember.'

Sarah continued. 'What did the van look like?'

'It was white and had "Express Cleaning" on the side. The windows were tinted so I couldn't see the driver. I wish I could tell you more. Wait a minute. There was something. Before the young guy started crossing, I saw him wave to a man on the opposite side. The man waved back and then disappeared.'

Sarah continued the questioning. 'Would you be able to recognize that man?'

'I wouldn't be able to recognize his face but from a distance he looked like an important businessman.'

'What do you mean by an important businessman?' Sarah asked.

'He was wearing a fancy looking suit.'

Sarah was curious. 'How do you know it was fancy?'

'It looked like a suit the attorneys wear on the Avenue of the Americas.'

Sarah looked up from her notebook. 'Was there anything else you noticed about the guy who was wearing the fancy looking suit? For example, was he Caucasian, black?'

'He wasn't black; I know that much.'

'What about his height. Do you think he was taller, shorter, or the same height as you?'

'He was definitely taller than me and was slim. The traffic blocked some of my view, but he had short fair hair and was an older guy. Probably around his forties and...he stroked the front of his hair.'

'We need you to come down to the station to go through

some mugshots. You may be able to recognize someone. It might take up a good part of the day,' James said.

'I'm glad to help you man, but I really need to work. I'm struggling with money as it is. I've got mouths to feed.'

James took out his wallet. 'Here, this'll cover your costs for the day; on one condition. Will you make me a mean hotdog?'

'I sell the best hotdogs in New York, you can ask anyone.'

'James, you'll get us into trouble.' Sarah raised her eyebrows and lowered her tone. 'That could be perceived as positively swaying an eyewitness.'

James looked like the cat that ate the canary. 'I know, I know. I couldn't help but compensate the guy.'

Sarah grinned. 'I understand the context and intention, but we'll just keep your kind act under wraps.'

James could tell George was a good person. It was easy for someone to witness a crime and then walk away thinking someone else would help. He'd spoken with witnesses who'd had to live with their guilt because they hadn't reported something suspicious or they'd only done so days later when it was too late for the victim.

'There's one more thing, George,' James said. 'What made you call us?'

'If it happened to me, I'd hope someone would help.'

'Ok, thanks George. Now, where's that mean hotdog?' James asked.

James turned to Sarah and said quietly, 'Interesting. Our man on the street corner strokes his hair just like our Doctor Ellison and matches his height. He also wears a fancy suit. Interesting. I wonder if it's Ellison's hand-tailored suit.'

Sarah nodded. She then dated her last entry and closed her notebook. She knew that George's eyewitness testimony might not hold up in court due to his distance from the crime, but she thanked the power of good for getting one step closer to an evil predator.

THIRTY

PROPAGANDA

Pastor Sleeman considered himself a wealthy genius. He'd progressed from high school dropout to powerful pastor who brainwashed his submissive followers.

Born with a club foot, he had worn calipers until he was seven years old. Throughout his adult years, the scars of schoolyard teasing remained. He could still hear their taunting: *'Here comes the cripple, here comes the cripple! Quick! Run and hide, run and hide or you'll catch his germs!'*

Due to his parents' guilt over their son's disability, they'd emotionally overcompensated and frequently told him he was special. He became isolated from other children and despised their happiness. Feeling powerless as a child had driven his psychopathic fantasies. *'One day I'll show them I'm not just some dumb cripple. My IQ is one of the highest and they know it. They will burn in hell. They will be sorry,'* he'd promised himself.

Many of his followers had been outcasts of society and were desperate to fit in and belong to a family. The pastor knew the power of words when preaching to the masses. 'I work hard for God and not for reward. It is more blessed to give than to receive. Let us save the people of Vegas.' His worshippers happily gave him whatever dollars they had in the hope that they would have everlasting salvation.

He knew how easily they submitted and obeyed him. Not only did they hand over their bank accounts, but the elderly also named him in their wills. He had gained an empire of wealth from those who were desperately lonely and looking for salvation. His cash flow provided a luxurious lifestyle which included a hotel, golf course, penthouses, and even a private jet, all tax deductible. He told his parishioners that thanks to their generous donations, his jet helped him spread the word of God.

He promoted group discussions rather than individual inter-actions, a successful strategy he had found in his research into Adolf Hitler's speeches. Anyone who had challenged Hitler's ideals had been quickly overruled by others in the group.

The pastor's followers feared retribution and alienation by speaking against him. He told them that rejecting God and his commandments led to decay and corruption of mankind. The guilt of rebellion kept his congregation faithful.

The pastor considered his worshippers were like ants march-ing under his control. He would not hesitate to kill anyone who challenged him. He knew they feared him and feared burning in hell. This opened the path to submission and wealth.

He relished the thought of becoming the U.S. president and living in the White House, with like-minded leaders, while recruiting his loyal and billionaire business associates for his mission of revenge on those who'd gone against him. They would be squashed like a bug and women would be at his mercy but for now, he had toys that provided him power and fun. His favorites were kept in a basement he called his "toy box." The church provided him with the perfect vessel for evil, along with the opportunity to satisfy his lustful games. He knew only that his toys came from a Mr X in Manhattan.

When the pastor ordered his toys, the victims were deliv-ered to The Lord's House of Therapy. The younger the toy, the higher the price.

His hands trembled at the thought of his next toy. Murder was his dessert on the menu. He considered himself the chosen one, entitled to have anyone he desired. He was no longer the cripple. He was the one who enjoyed the vulnerability and helplessness of his victims.

No one suspected the pastor. Despite not being Catholic, he had been an honorary guest at the Vatican where he had been awarded a medal for his work with the homeless.

The pastor was married to his teenage sweetheart, Magda, and they had one daughter, Helga. He loved to spoil his daughter and never missed a chance to play the role of doting and devoted dad at any school or family event. To outsiders, he looked like the typical family man.

When the pastor wasn't available for church functions, he justified to his followers, 'I could work all day and night, but I value my beautiful family and being a good husband and father means spending precious time with them.'

The pastor separated his predatory life from his family life, switching roles seamlessly. He owned a home for his family and The Lord's House of Therapy, where he told everyone he conducted spiritual healing through music and dance. His family never visited The Lord's House of Therapy; this was a strict rule. It was just one of a long list of rules that had to be obeyed. No one dared go against his rules.

* * *

In the beginning, Magda had revered her husband. She had even changed her name from Lorna to Magda at his request. He'd said Magda was a strong name that bestowed wisdom, courage, and positive values. She helped support his beliefs but there were times when she had an underlying fear for her safety. The fear travelled from her throat to the pit of her stomach.

Magda was clever at hiding her true feelings and playing the loyal and happy wife. She knew that no one would understand her fear, as her husband was so skilled at manipulating others. She considered him more like a cult figure whose words would cast an evil spell for control. She knew that she would look like a liar if she ever said anything against him. At social gatherings, he would often say, 'I have a beautiful family and staff who work tirelessly for others burdened with life stressors. I am proud of them all.'

She knew the chilling truth behind the seemingly benign words and overly positive manner. She often experienced his sudden and frightening anger. When she disagreed with him, he squeezed his fingers around her neck. What she didn't know was his murderous personality. A personality type that could kill her. A personality type that could squeeze the life out of her.

* * *

The pastor was preparing for his next toy at The Lord's House of Therapy when he heard the buzzer from the front security gates. The routine was always the same and his excitement built.

'Yes?' the Pastor asked.

'Your package has arrived, Sir.'

'You know the drill.' He opened the gates.

Max was the best driver around. He did his job with no questions asked and the toys always arrived in one piece.

* * *

Max preferred to work alone, as snitching was always a danger, but with a street grab he didn't have a choice but to hire help. His golden rule was to drop off his accomplice, with a wad of cash in his pocket, and then head to Vegas to make his delivery.

Max drove down into the basement garage at The Lord's House of Therapy with practiced ease. He stepped out of the van and stretched, feeling relief at completing another assignment without a glitch.

The van appeared empty except for a few cardboard boxes. The metal flooring of the van was an illusion. He unclipped two levers and pulled out a false floor that looked like an oblong toolbox. This was no ordinary toolbox. It was designed with a mesh grid that allowed enough airflow for the victim. The toy wasn't making a noise. There was no room to kick and fight. Instead, he was frozen with fear.

Although Max considered himself detached from the suffering of the pastor's victims, he did not consider himself a cold-blooded killer. He justified to himself that if he didn't do the job, someone else would. His courier work provided him a lifestyle that others could only dream of. He had a beach house on the Californian coast, his kids went to the best schools, and his wife lived a life of extravagance. Because of this, he could depersonalize the victims and detach from any feelings for them.

His family was oblivious to his contradictory values. After a delivery, Max always looked forward to seeing his wife, Kimberly, and his two children, Sofia and Lilly, who giggled with delight on his arrival and tore around the house playing tag, oblivious to the disturbing real-life games Daddy played.

His wife thought he worked as a Secret Service agent for the Department of Homeland Security. His job justified spending weekends away when any of the presidential family went on vacation. She'd accepted his story without question, explaining to family, friends and social acquaintances her husband's regular absences by saying he looked after their investment properties. She kept her word and never discussed her husband's secret assignments with anyone, until she found a diner docket from Vegas with a date that didn't match his story. He was supposed to be in Washington DC, working in the Oval Office but according to the docket, he'd been eating at Stallone's Burger Bar in Vegas. Kimberly remembered his call that weekend. He'd told her about the Washington blizzard and how slippery the roads were. She knew his work was top secret, but she didn't expect him to lie about his location, and lie so convincingly.

Now Kimberly wondered whether to hire a private investigator to see if he was hiding a dirty little secret.

THIRTY-ONE

MEGALOMANIA

Mohsen was busy distributing food parcels on the streets of Vegas and running his food kitchen. He was the imam of a mosque on the outskirts of Vegas, a charitable man who worked in the seedy Vegas alleyways and back streets helping the needy, away from the tourists who were mesmerized by the glitz and glamour of the Vegas strip.

He recruited young Muslims and non-Muslims as volunteers to teach them the value of helping others and to foster a healthy sense of identity. Building cultural and religious bridges for world peace and unity was something Mohsen believed in. He encouraged young Muslims to integrate and harmonize with other youths their age who were non-Islamic, so they wouldn't feel alienated or isolated because of their religion.

Being Muslim wasn't easy in Vegas. Occasionally he was spat on, but he held no grudges and didn't judge anyone for being afraid. He knew it worked several ways. There were non-Muslims who feared Muslims, Muslims who feared non-Muslims, and Muslims who feared Muslims. He didn't think too much about it. He considered life was too sweet to dwell on negativity.

As he walked along the Vegas strip, a vehicle screeched to a halt. He stepped behind a bus shelter, hoping not to be seen.

A vehicle door opened, a young girl fell out onto the sidewalk. She looked no more than twenty years old. No one stopped to help. It was as if she was invisible. She was crying and there was blood smeared under her nose.

Before the vehicle sped off, Mohsen caught a glimpse of a man sitting in the back seat. He was sure it was pastor Sleeman, who he'd met at a charity dinner. Pastor Sleeman was the founder of the Vegas Savior's Church. He had over two thousand followers who came for salvation every week. Among his followers were gamblers, sex addicts, alcoholics, drug addicts, and anyone else who needed saving. Some were eternally trapped in Vegas, like mice on a treadmill, making enough money to escape but unable to resist their lust for another gamble. Vegas provided the perfect environment to nurture their cycle of addiction.

Mohsen knew that pastor Sleeman called Las Vegas the devil's euphoria and reassured his worshippers they had the power to change their lives and receive what he called 'religious ecstasy', promising a shift from the devil's strip to true enlightenment. The sign on his vehicle read, 'The Lord God is the only truth.' Pastor Sleeman preached morals and the evil of gambling to the most vulnerable. He spoke of redemption, forgiveness, and everlasting life.

What does pastor Sleeman have to do with this girl? Mohsen wondered. Her arms were outstretched as she balanced on her heels, trying to get up. She wiped the tears and blood from her face as the vehicle sped off.

Mohsen recognized her. It was Bella. She worked at a strip club and he had seen her using drugs. The last time he had spoken to her, she was trying hard to kick the habit.

'Are you ok? Can I help you?' Mohsen asked.

'I don't need your help. I'm ok.'

'Who was that man? Did he hurt you?'

'Why do you care? No one else cares,' she replied, her voice trembling.

'I care because you have a right to be safe. If someone is doing this to you it has to be stopped. Please, take this food.'

Bella could see the goodness in his eyes. She couldn't understand why he cared and why he didn't see her as trash.

'My wife can take you to a safe house tonight.'

'No, it won't do any good. That client is dangerous. I've tried to get away before and he ends up finding me. It's no use fighting it. You don't understand.'

Mohsen had seen it before. The girls were stripped of their self-worth and identity. Unless someone physically took them off the streets, they were forever trapped by their perpetrator's emotional and violent control.

'Was that man in the back seat the pastor?' asked Mohsen.

'Yes. He's dangerous and totally untouchable. He said he's entitled to do whatever he wants because he owns me. He has lots of money and knows lots of people.' As she spoke, she looked around fearfully.

'But Bella, how do you know the pastor?'

'The owner of my strip club told me that he knew a pastor who could help me get off the drugs. I went to church and met him. He said he was God's overseer and he called me the chosen one. He said I had to fulfil my destiny by satisfying God's overseer. He beats me if I don't follow his orders. How could I have believed him! How could I be so stupid.'

'You're not stupid. He betrayed your trust in the worst possible way. This man doesn't define who you are. You must go to the police.'

'The pastor mixes with people in high places. He can shut anyone up with money. He brags about his hush money. You don't understand. He doesn't drop off food parcels; he drops off...bodies.'

'How do you know he drops off bodies, Bella?' Mohsen asked, trying not to sound too alarmed.

'He takes me down to a room underneath his Lord's House of Therapy to play his games. Today, I heard a boy crying behind the walls of his basement. He must have heard me. He kept saying, "He's going to kill me. My name is Sean Young. I'm from Manhattan. I was abducted. Please help me! He's going to kill me." He called out over and over. He wouldn't shut up. It was horrible. My mind went blank and I didn't know what to do. He's now in my head begging for help. I did nothing to help him. I deserve to be punished by God. I am evil. I belong in hell just like the Bible says.'

'Bella, you did what was necessary to survive. He is the evil one. If he is hurting people, he will not get a whiff of heaven.'

'But if I feel evil, I must be evil,' Bella cried.

'Don't always trust your feelings. If you feel like you're dying, it doesn't mean it's true. Please listen to me. He's got to be stopped. You have to call the police,' Mohsen begged. 'If you can't do it, I will.'

'You've got to be kidding! Haven't you looked at yourself lately? A Muslim hasn't a chance in hell of reporting anyone, especially a pastor. Don't you know what's happening in the world? You'll be skinned alive. Look around you. People are already looking you up and down and wondering why you're talking to me. They're suspicious as hell.'

Before Bella walked away, she looked at Mohsen with concern. 'If he's ever caught, I'll think about being a witness but in the meantime, don't ask any more questions. This pastor has many like-minded followers. They follow him like sheep and they'd do anything to protect him. I've heard he's received a medal from the Pope and he's not even catholic so please go away or we'll both end up dead. I might not be smart enough to get a real job, but I do know one thing.'

'And what's that?' Mohsen asked.

'This man...'

'Yes Bella, what is it?'

Bella's eyes opened wide with fear. 'He's evil wrapped in skin.'

Mohsen understood her fear. He knew she was right about everything she'd said. What concerned him the most was that right now; a boy was being held captive in pastor Sleeman's basement.

THIRTY-TWO

PLOTTING DESTRUCTION

Dr Cameron canceled his afternoon appointments and gave his personal assistant, Jennifer, the afternoon off. He stroked his curly white beard and removed his glasses, rubbing his tired eyes. He had returned from his health and well-being conference faced with an ethical dilemma regarding complaints from two of his clients.

* * *

Jennifer thought her boss looked more like Father Christmas than a psychiatrist, his white bushy eyebrows and gentle blue eyes reflecting a kind heart. He insisted that she call him Lee, not Doctor. There wasn't a trace of arrogance in his manner. She loved working for him, although she was delighted to be able to leave early. Her previous boss had been a bully. He had made her feel worthless and stupid. The more he belittled her, the more mistakes she'd made. She'd suffered severe anxiety attacks. It was only by luck she'd noticed the advertisement for Lee's personal assistant.

She cleared the last papers on her desk, locked the filing cabinet, and popped her head around Lee's office door. 'I'm going now Lee, are you sure there's nothing else I can do?'

'Not at all, you go on home. I need to catch up on some paperwork. Enjoy your evening.'

'Call me if there's anything you need. You know I'd be back in a flash.'

He didn't look up and his eyes remained fixed on a client's file.

Although Jennifer was happy to leave early, she noticed he was not his usual self.

'Is everything alright, Lee?'

'Oh yes, yes, I've just got a lot on my mind, but nothing too serious.'

'Ok, see you in the morning,' Jennifer responded.

She didn't want to ask too many questions and appear to be prying into his personal business. She accepted that running a private practice wasn't an easy job and some days were more challenging than others. Without giving it another thought, she hurried out of the building.

* * *

Once Jennifer had left, Lee meticulously went through a couple of his clients' notes, word by word, reading and re-reading case notes until he was satisfied there was a pattern – and a disturbing connection between their stories. He then made an internal call to his colleague Ellison.

Doctor Ellison noticed the internal buzzer light and wondered why Lee was calling.

'Hi Lee, how can I help?'

'I'm finishing up for the day but I'm wondering if you're free for a chat before I go home?'

'What's up?' he asked.

'It's about something that's concerning me. Two of your former clients have accused you of professional misconduct. They're claiming sexual harassment and some sort of new therapy you wanted them to participate in.'

Dr Ellison was skilled at not sounding rattled. 'I don't quite understand why it's a concern of yours if it's regarding ex-clients of mine? Just refer them back to me.'

'Maybe we can discuss this further,' Lee said. 'I'm free now, if you are?'

'I'm sure it's all just a misunderstanding. I'll be there in ten minutes,' Ellison replied.

'Ok, see you then.'

Therapy to Lee was about self-regulating and self-healing change. What he was hearing from Dr Ellison's clients was forced participation in a therapy without their consent. He was also concerned about the clients' ordering of unregulated medication and herbal drinks off the internet. Lee knew if it wasn't for Dr Ellison he wouldn't have his job, so it was only fair to give him the opportunity to explain the alleged misconduct.

Lee poured himself a coffee and waited for his colleague to arrive.

* * *

Ellison swung around in his chair, wondering how to eliminate the problem. He contacted his next client and moved the appointment an hour ahead.

He accessed Lee's appointments on the database. There was a client, Daniel Mackie, who had seen Lee at 2.00 pm. It took seconds to open the client's file. It stated he was twenty-two, lived alone, was unemployed, and was diagnosed with paranoid schizophrenia.

The doctor knew that the public's irrational fears of anyone with mental illness would be enough to see Daniel as a likely suspect.

He downloaded a mental health assessment form.

He typed:

Paranoid Schizophrenia: The client exhibits inco-
herent, illogical thoughts and behaviors. He is also
experiencing thought insertion and has made several
threats against my life. He believes I am stalking him
and states a higher being has given him orders to kill
me. He was extremely agitated during the therapy
session and paced around the room. The client has
exhibited intermittent outbursts of anger. The client
has stopped taking his anti-psychotic drugs due to his
belief that I am poisoning him.

An emergency hospital admission is required for
immediate observation, care and treatment, due to
this client having a mental illness that is likely to
result in serious harm to himself or others. The client
is to be kept in psychiatric care until assessed.

He attached the completed assessment form to Daniel's file
on the database. He then carefully put on his surgical gloves
and printed it out. Without wasting any time, he tucked it into
the inside pocket of his jacket and whispered evilly, 'Thank
you, Daniel. You don't know how much this means to me.'

The doctor reached under his desk and unlocked a hidden
compartment. As it opened, it revealed a long, double-bladed
knife. He smirked and held the knife in the air to admire its
sharp edge. He carefully slipped the knife into the back of his
suit pants, held securely by his belt.

He considered this would be an easy job; no one would
suspect him. He relished in the fantasy of the kill and antici-
pated the newspaper headline: *'Severely disturbed schizophrenic
client stabs psychiatrist to death in psychotic and delusional rage.'*

He gave a sinister smile at the thought of being the master
of deception. 'You fuckin' asshole, Lee,' he sneered.

THIRTY-THREE

FIRST DEGREE NARCISSISM

Wanting to avoid the CCTV, the doctor took the internal stairs up to the fifth floor. A nerve beneath his eye twitched, as it had done on the day of his stepbrother's death. He entered Lee's reception area.

He felt the knife press against his back as he knocked on Lee's door.

'Come on in, Luke. I'm glad you could see me.'

There was an awkward silence as Lee produced two files.

'Two clients, Ashley and Kayla, have complained about your therapy sessions.'

'They're delusional. You know what it's like, Lee. Patients splitting between their therapists and making false accusations. I'm the bad cop and now you're the good cop. The clients you're talking about have bipolar and borderline personality.'

'Yes. They have bipolar and bpd. I'm not understanding where this is going, Luke.'

'Surely you know the code for these pathological liars?'

'Sorry? I'm still not following you, Luke.'

'I'm talking about the three Cs. Complaints, chaos, and conflict! You know very well their insatiable need for validation and their propensity for doctor-shopping. I may have set ethical boundaries that they found intolerable. They love you one moment and hate you the next, along with their faking bad and playing the fucking suicide game.'

'What about caring and compassion? These clients are unwell. Furthermore, a client has the right to feel safe and to be supported. You know perfectly well it's about protecting the client,' Lee responded.

'Don't give me that ethical bullshit as if I'm some fuckin' deviant. They blame everyone else for their fuck-ups. We are their perfect target. Anyway, clients lie for sympathy and let's not forget – everyone's raped them except the mailman!'

'That is totally out of line!'

'I'm sorry if you're in denial about your client's Lee. For God's sake get real. They're skilled malingerers. They'd hang us from a tree if they could.'

'So, what I'm hearing now, your clients have made up identical stories because of their bpd. Is that correct?'

'I'm not following you Lee. What is your point?'

'My point is, you are giving advice to undergo an unknown experimental treatment called cognitive environment therapy. From what they've said, there was no informed consent and you expected them to comply and do this therapy in Central Park. They also stated you gave them a psychological questionnaire called the CET Mental Health Test. You told them their score meant they were highly delusional. Is this test of yours valid?'

'Are you done with your humorous journey of ethics?'

'No, I haven't. The clients have stopped their antidepressants and are now taking unregulated herbal drinks and vitamins off the internet on your advice. Surely, you're aware of how dangerous this can be?'

'For fuck's sake Lee, these pharmaceutical companies are laughing their way to the bank with their screwed-up antidepressants. It's just another money-grubbing rort. Anyway, if the clients are going to Central Park for therapy and they expect it to work, then it's going to fuckin' work. Don't tell me you've forgotten the placebo effect. You're getting forgetful in your old age, Lee. Maybe you need a chill pill.'

'Don't treat me like an old fool! You really think you have the right to take clients off their medication and push your own agenda? These clients are exceptionally intelligent and remembered exactly what you have told them so don't bother minimizing their complaints and presenting them as incompetent. I'm not brushing this under the carpet.'

'It sounds like you've made up your mind. I'm done with explaining,' Ellison responded.

'You leave me with no choice but to report your behavior to the Board of Ethics and unless you can convince me otherwise, I will be contacting them first thing in the morning.'

'You think you're so smart, don't you Lee,' Ellison sneered. 'You think you can throw me under the bus because of your bloody ethics when in fact you're just a joke, a nobody. A fuckin' weak lapdog.'

Lee stood up. 'How dare you speak to me like that! You are despicable! This conversation is finished. Your behavior with clients is not only unethical, it's putting them at risk. Get out of my office now!' Lee's face flushed with anger.

Ellison rested one hand on his hip while pointing a finger at Lee. 'Don't fuckin' lecture me about client boundaries. You're forgetting one thing, Lee. I got you this job after you fucked up on professional misconduct. Who was the one who got their license revoked? Who was the one who had to do a boundaries course? Remember, Lee? You were the one who fucked your client and I was the one who got you off that fuckin' hook.'

Lee leaned forward whilst resting both hands on his desk. 'I've been through five years of hell regretting that one night. My wife doesn't speak to me and my children refuse to see me. Regardless of what I have done in the past, you cannot continue your abuse of clients.'

Ellison's fingers wrapped around the handle of his knife. 'The one thing I love about transparency Lee, people like you experience my unmasked self.'

Lee gave Ellison a perplexed look before reaching for his cell.

Ellison slipped the knife from his belt and lunged forward. Lee was a sitting duck. The sharp blade pierced his chest with ease and precision. Lee reeled in shock as he felt the coolness of the blade enter his chest and then a searing pain. His eyes opened wide in bewilderment.

Ellison yanked the client files from his grip. 'Thank you, Lee. I appreciate you giving me these files. Their complaints will die with you. Why are you looking so surprised? You really think I was going to walk out of here and let you ruin my life? You're a weak old man and I must say, feeble-minded. Now look who's delusional!' He laughed. 'And sorry about your family, shit happens.'

Lee gasped for breath while clutching his chest. As he fell forward, he caught sight of his family portrait. Taking his last breath, he prayed his family would forgive him.

Ellison watched as Lee slumped to the ground. He stepped over his body with callous indifference. 'You're pathetic, Lee. A high-grade moron.' He pulled the knife from Lee's chest and placed it in a plastic bag.

The doctor had twenty minutes before his next client arrived. She would provide the perfect alibi. He put Daniel's assessment form on Lee's desk and made his way down the stairwell clutching Lee's files. He thought it an easy job. As he returned to his office, he saw his client flicking through a magazine. *Damn it!* he thought. *Of all times, she's early for her appointment.*

'Hello, Mrs Moore. You're early.'

'I was shopping in the area, so I thought it wouldn't hurt to be early.'

'I won't be long; would you like a glass of water while you wait?'

'No thank you,' she replied.

It wouldn't be an airtight alibi now, but it would have to do.

'Excuse me, Doctor?'

'Yes?'

'I think you have a spot of blood on your collar.'

'Oh yes, I had a nosebleed earlier. This heat gets me every time. I won't be a moment. I'll just freshen up.' He was furious. Not only had she seen him enter from the stairwell, she had also seen the blood. He wanted to snap her neck and watch the blood ooze from her eyes, but he resisted the urge.

He loathed Mrs Moore. She was a sixty-year-old whose voice was grating and who stank of roses. She had tough wrinkled breasts that were pushed up high, and her dress was wrapped around her thighs like a bandage. He dreaded her weekly sessions. It was difficult to keep up with her incessant dialogue. Her jaws slapped up and down while saliva built up in the corners of her mouth. If it wasn't for her money, her driveling would be unbearable. Her husband was a stockbroker who had bought out several large companies during a market crash. Once the market recovered, his shares skyrocketed, and he made a killing.

During their session, as usual, she hardly paused for breath. This provided time for the doctor to plan his next move. He heard every siren and alarm outside the building, and had to force himself to sit still. He wondered whether Lee's body had been found. He hoped he had time to get to the client's house.

After Mrs Moore left, he drove thirty minutes out of the city until he reached the small town of Vetrilli. It looked like the typical quiet community with its tree-lined streets and picket fences. A place where parents had the illusion that a small country town meant safety for their children. He wondered how many killers were concealed behind the pretty little fences, their victims providing fertilizer for their manicured gardens.

He remembered a client who had confessed to killing his mother. *I grew tired of looking after my mom, so I popped some extra sleeping pills in her morning juice. It was as easy as that. I then dismembered her and placed her in our garden mulcher, reducing her to blood and bone for the vegetable patch.* He'd told the neighbors she was in a nursing home. Fortunately for him, his mother was a recluse and had enjoyed life with her animals and garden. He forged her signature on the house documents and became the proud owner of a quaint cottage by the lake.

Client stories provided the doctor with pleasurable reflections.

He parked the vehicle and walked the rest of the distance to 24 Oakwood Drive. Luck was on his side. The night was moonless and there were no cars in the driveway. He wondered whether the client had a car, but thought it more likely he caught public transport and would be home.

He edged his way alongside the house, gingerly taking a step at a time. Hearing a slight sound, he stopped, listening, tilting his head to one side. A neighbor's dog was going ballistic. Its rapid repetitive barking could only mean one thing: *Warning, an intruder is on our property!*

He saw the neighbor's back light flick on and heard a swing door slamming. He then heard footsteps approaching.

'Shut up, you useless, good-for-nothing dog.'

The neighbor stumbled back to the house, crashing into a trash can. 'Fuckin' can and fuckin' dog.' The old drunk didn't have a clue he was a couple of feet away from a killer.

Fuckin' piss-head, the doctor thought. He remained crouched. The neighbor slammed his door, still cussing. The doctor stepped slowly to the back door. It should be an easy job. He jiggled a piece of wire in the back lock. The sound of a click was music to his ears.

He made his way through the wooden home until he reached the client's bedroom. The door was shut, and he could see a light peeping from under the door. He heard someone mumbling and pacing. Without wasting time, he made his way to the living room where he surreptitiously placed the blood-ied knife under the client's couch. *How easy it is to fool them all,* he thought.

THIRTY-FOUR

TRIGGER-HAPPY

It was 9.00 am when James got his wakeup call.

'Hi James, it's Sarah. I know it's early, but we have another dead body.'

'Jesus! Who this time?' James asked.

'We have a dead psychiatrist. It's the doctor's colleague, Dr Lee Cameron. He was found on his office floor this morning. He'd been stabbed in the chest. From the look on his face, he wasn't expecting it. The body is in full rigor mortis which means he could have been killed yesterday afternoon. I'm waiting on the time of death from the coroner's office. There goes one of our suspects.'

'Who found him?' James asked.

'His personal assistant found him this morning. I'm on my way there now to interview her.'

James felt a shot of adrenalin. *Retirement doesn't give me this feeling,* he thought.

'What about Dr Ellison?'

'He's already been interviewed. Apparently, he was with clients all afternoon.'

By 10.00 am, they were ready to interview Dr Cameron's assistant. She was sitting at the front desk crying, with a handkerchief pressed against her mouth.

'Hello Jennifer, I'm Sarah and this is James. We're from the New York Police Department.'

Jennifer nodded as tears rolled down her cheeks.

'We know this is an extremely stressful time for you but unfortunately, we do have to ask you a few questions. Do you know anyone who might want to hurt the doctor?'

'Absolutely not. He was the kindest man in the world. I don't understand why anyone would hurt him.'

'Did you notice anything unusual happening in the last couple of days? Did he seem a little different, or was there something you noticed with any of his clients?'

'Not that I can think of. He was a little agitated yesterday afternoon, that's all.'

'What do you mean by agitated?' James asked.

'He just didn't seem himself and he said I could leave early. I didn't want to pry but now I wished I had.'

'Can we see his appointments for the week?'

Jennifer opened Lee's calendar on the computer. 'Here are all his appointments.'

Sarah peered at the screen and saw he was fully booked. 'Can we take his laptop to check his clients?'

'Of course.' Jennifer then scribbled a code on a piece of paper. 'Here's the doctor's password if you want to access any of his files, emails, or his patient appointments. I wish I could help you more. I hope you get the monster who did this.'

'Thanks for your help, Jennifer. We'll call you if we need any further information.'

James scanned Doctor Cameron's office. He noticed a client's mental health assessment form on the doctor's desk labeled 'Daniel Mackie'. He put on his gloves and carefully picked up the form. 'Looks like we've got something here,' he said quietly. 'According to this assessment, a client called Daniel Mackie threatened his life. He's been diagnosed with paranoid schizophrenia. It may be worth checking him out.'

He turned the form over and added, 'Well, well, what have we here?'

'What's up?' Sarah asked.

'There's no blood on the front of the form but blood marks on the back. It's been placed on the desk after the doctor was stabbed.'

'Someone wants us to read this,' Sarah said.

'That's what I'm thinking.' James looked at Doctor Cameron's appointments. 'And from what I can see here, the doctor saw Daniel Mackie at 2.00 pm. Looks pretty sus. Daniel's assessment form sitting on the doctor's desk screaming *Read me! Read me! I'm a client with the means, the motive, and the opportunity.* Sounds too convenient.'

'Interesting,' Sarah responded. 'Something doesn't fit. If this client is the murderer, how did he know when the Doctor had finished with clients and that his assistant had left early? Did he re-enter the building and take a chance, or did he stay hidden somewhere in the building until he knew the doctor was on his own? How about we pay this client, Daniel Mackie, a visit and in the meantime, I'll get the boys to check the building's CCTV footage.'

'Good idea,' James responded.

It was still early when they hit the road to the suspect's house. Sarah let her team drive ahead. She hadn't had breakfast, so a quick drive-through meal would do.

'Do me a favor James.' Sarah pointed to a left turn. 'There's a Burger King drive-thru. Can you get me a burger?'

'You live on takeaway Sarah.'

'It's quick and easy. I'm too busy to cook...anyway, one day when I get out of this job, I'll make some changes.'

It didn't take long for Sarah to devour her vegan burger and skull a soy latte.

'Where's your favorite bacon burger?'

'I've changed my eating habits. I became a cop. Meat reminds me of our victims. Our victims cry before they're killed. Cows cry before they're killed. I can't eat an animal that's suffered because of me. Besides, I had a case where a killer skinned his victim alive, just like skinning an animal for its hide when it's still kicking. I can't stomach the thought of...'

Sarah was interrupted by the crackle of her radio. She received the worse possible news. Daniel Mackie was dead. He was gardening at the back of his property when he saw the cops and charged them with a garden tool. A rookie shot him on the spot. Not only that, it wasn't one of her boys. He was a temporary fill-in. Her stomach sank. She couldn't believe her ears.

'Jesus, they probably scared the hell out of him. I told them he had schizophrenia. I didn't want him dead. What were they thinking?' Sarah was fuming. 'Why the hell had they gone in like Robocops with guns blazing? I can't believe a rookie, who knows stuff-all about mental illness, took out a possibly innocent man and why the hell didn't I know about this temporary fill-in?' Sarah closed her eyes as she processed the news.

'It's bad enough he had mental health issues but thank God he wasn't black,' James responded.

Sarah looked at James and let out an exasperated sigh. 'With everything going on in the media lately I don't think it will matter who it is. The media will be after us like bloodhounds. Our credibility is shot as it is without this fuck-up and how the hell do I explain this to his family? I feel like I fired the bullet. I feel like absolute shit.'

'You feel like shit because you care Sarah and you're a good cop.'

'Well, I'm not feeling like a good cop. I'm picturing him getting killed for minding his own business and enjoying his garden whilst I'm crapping on about myself. If only I'd got there sooner. If only I'd missed breakfast. Bloody drive-thru. I could have waited.'

'Don't go blaming yourself. You've been working around the clock and you've got to eat.'

'Why there aren't screening tests that weed out these bloody rogue rookies who think they are the judge, jury and executioner. Now, I can smell a rat and this one stinks. The doctor's colleague ends up murdered and a client is now the dead suspect. A client with suspected paranoid schizophrenia is an easy target to frame. It's just all too easy, don't you think James?'

'Definitely.'

'And speaking of rats, I'm betting Dr Cameron was going to rat on his colleague. Now I'm facing another dead end and I've got a massive headache. I need some pain killers and your inspiration James.'

'With Dr Ellison as our prime suspect, I think it's time to get a snapshot of his past and pay his mom a visit. What do you think?' James asked.

'Let's do it,' Sarah responded. 'She lives in a retirement home on Long Island. From what I can remember the home is in Southampton.'

'What about other family members?'

'Dr Ellison is her only child. From our records, he lived with his mom, stepdad, and stepbrother on a farm during his childhood.'

'Where does his stepbrother live now?'

'Nowhere,' Sarah replied. 'He was accidentally killed on a camping trip. He fell off a ridge...and that's not all, the doctor's stepdad allegedly suicided.'

James reached for his notebook. 'Death surrounds this psychologist. His stepbrother falls off a ridge, his stepdad shoots himself, and now his colleague is found lying in a pool of blood. This guy either has a lot of bad luck, or he's a habitual killer. When do we leave to speak to his mother?'

'I'll interview this gun happy rookie and break the sad news to Daniel's family, then I'll organize a chopper to take us to Long Island.'

'Sounds good to me,' James responded.

THIRTY-FIVE

AUTOMATIC ASSOCIATIONS

The chopper was on its way from the Floyd Bennett Field to the precinct rooftop where Sarah and James stood waiting. The commissioner had approved the use of his 'baby', a Bell 412EP helicopter costing over $9,000,000, carrying top-secret weapons worth more than $4,000,000. It was not only the fastest chopper in New York, but it was also a smooth ride. The chopper was equipped to fight local crime and designed for counter-terrorism.

The chopper was a beauty and so was the pilot. Kate had been piloting for ten years and oversaw the NYPD's navigation team. She was not only smart but also drop-dead gorgeous. There wasn't a male member of the force who didn't want her. Both her father and grandfather had been cops with bravery medals to their name, so the force was in her blood.

Sarah had a fear of flying and heights, but she trusted Kate. If they had to land on a tin roof, Kate could do it. Sarah had to fly almost every week, but she still felt breathless as her heart beat pounded her chest. No matter how much she rationalized her fear, she always second guessed whether she was having a heart attack. She wondered whether it was a fear inherited from her ancestor's experiences. *If personality can be predisposed, why not a fear of heights?* she thought. Then she realized she sounded like James.

She and James strapped themselves in and Kate gave Sarah a reassuring nod. In seconds, Kate was flying the team to Southampton at a hundred and thirty miles per hour. The Hudson River shimmered with reflections of the city's skyscrapers and the city looked more like a toy town.

Sarah focused on her mission and tightened her seat belt as they flew over Ellis Island and past the Statue of Liberty. As a child, she remembered climbing Liberty's spiral metal stairway on a school excursion. It was a time to mess around and show off. Her class climbed to the top in single file to the crown. *Happy memories,* she thought. She fixed her gaze on the Lady, silently asking for her help.

She dreamed of having a vacation without the presence of death and paperwork. She imagined herself in a Piazza, overlooking an ocean of endless blue and enjoying homemade pasta and red wine. She promised to take better care of herself. Her work had taken its toll and she needed time out. The last thing she wanted was to end up a basket case with post trauma.

Sarah was the first to admit her job came first, but she was yet to find a man who understood that. It wasn't the glass ceiling that made it difficult for her, it was more the lack of support once she was in a relationship. She noticed her male colleagues always acknowledged their families on award nights. *'I'd like to thank my wife and children for being there for me. This award wouldn't have been possible without them.'*

Was there a man out there who would support her career? She envied her colleagues' relationships but refused to dwell on them self-pityingly. In the end, she convinced herself she didn't need a man, it was a waste of time and energy. Her rap sheet for relationships were full of heartache. Sarah wondered whether she lacked the ability to emotionally connect but for now, she didn't care. She enjoyed her life and nothing else mattered, she convinced herself.

Sarah adjusted her headpiece and took time to read her notes.

'You have some more information on Doctor Ellison, James?'

'Sure do.' James flicked through his notebook. 'The doctor has some very interesting hobbies.'

'What do you mean by interesting?' Sarah asked.

'Our Doctor Ellison is a collector of semi-automatics and a trophy hunter of the big cats. He spends his vacations in Africa and the rest of his spare time at a shooting range. I wonder what his taste for hunting is when he's on home soil.'

'Anyone who kills wildlife for kicks is sick,' Sarah responded.

'I have something else that's interesting.' James handed over an FBI report.

'What is this?' Sarah asked.

'Evidence to prove that the doctor is an avid watcher of porn. The type of porn that is found on the dark web. There's nothing romantic or glamorous about the bondage he's been watching. The main star ends up snuffed off the planet.'

'I know they are still circulating but how did you manage to get your hands on this info?' asked Sarah.

'I have a friend in the FBI Cyber Division.'

'Having this FBI report is valuable for getting producers and suppliers, but his dark hobbies may not be enough to get a conviction,' Sarah said.

'We want a jury to know about his porn habit, trophy hunting and his collection of guns. Trophy hunters are void of empathy. Watching a snuff movie is no different. We want the jury to associate his hobbies with a killer who is living out his sick perversions by killing his clients.'

James gave a death stare beyond Sarah's face as if he was looking directly in the eyes of a killer. 'Our so-called squeaky-clean psychologist won't know what's hit him when I'm done. Capital punishment is too quick. I'm going to make sure that son of a bitch rots in a cell for the rest of his life. A prison for that bastard will be music to my ears. The first thing he'll see when he wakes up, will be his cell walls. The last thing he'll see when he goes to sleep will be those walls. He'll have a constant dose of his own medicine. A daily reminder he's in a cage, trapped forever.'

Sarah was relieved to have James on her team. His anger was productive. She needed his insight and energy to get their killer before he kills again. She knew the longer the killer was on the streets the longer the killing trail.

THIRTY-SIX

COMPASSIONATE LISTENING

Sarah and James had a smooth flight and their chopper landed on the grounds of the Kennedy Island Retirement Home in Southampton.

They ducked under the helicopter blades and walked to the historical mansion. A nurse was waiting to greet them.

'Welcome. I'm Lauren, Rose Ellison's nurse.'

'Hi Lauren. Nice to meet you. I'm Lieutenant Wilkins and this is Detective Christianson from the NYPD.'

'I was told you were on your way. It's not every day we get a helicopter landing on our lawn,' Lauren said.

Sarah looked up at the French chateau. 'And it's not every day I see a beautiful ocean mansion like this,' she said.

'It was built in 1915. The original owner made his fortune in the steel industry.'

'It's beautiful,' Sarah responded. 'Especially the stone terrace and rose garden.'

'Many of the mansions along here were demolished but lucky for us, this one was restored. The owner left it in his will as a retirement home.'

Sarah wondered what secrets were buried with the previous occupants and how the doctor could afford such a palatial retirement home for his mom.

'Rose is waiting for you. Come this way.'

Sarah and James followed Lauren along a pebbled pathway and to an oceanside gazebo. An elderly woman sat in a wheelchair with a crocheted rug neatly wrapped around her legs.

Lauren touched Rose's shoulder. 'Excuse me, Rose. I have the police officers from the New York Police Department who would like to speak with you.'

Rose looked up. 'Welcome. At last, I will have some excitement in my life,' she said with an infectious smile.

'I'm Lieutenant Wilkins and this is Detective James Christianson.'

'Glad to meet you, I'm Rose, and I've been on this earth too long,' she quipped.

'Let me know if you need anything, Rose,' Lauren said. 'I'll be back in ten minutes.'

'Thank you, Lauren, I will.'

As Lauren walked away, Rose moved her wheelchair to face Sarah and James. 'Please take a seat. There's no point standing around. Tell me, what is so important about my life that you needed a helicopter to come and see me?'

'We're hoping to ask you a few questions,' Sarah said.

'My body is tired, and words are difficult to find so I don't know whether I can be of much help.'

'It's about the death of your stepson Kevin.'

Rose sat up and straightened her shoulders. 'Why do you need to know anything about his death? It happened so long ago.'

'We would like to hear your version of events on the day he died.'

Rose looked surprised. 'No one ever asked me for my version of events.'

Sarah continued sensitively. 'Sorry to ask you these questions, Rose. I know it must be very distressing.'

Rose gave a deep sigh. 'I only wish it felt like a long time ago. It feels like it happened yesterday. A day doesn't go by that I don't think of that dreadful time. It weighs heavily on my heart. I was told that time heals. That's complete and utter nonsense. On that day, my world changed forever.'

'You lived with your husband Hank, your stepson Kevin, and your son Luke, is that correct?'

'Yes, that's right. My first husband walked out on Luke and me but then I met Hank, my second husband. Hank came from a broken relationship, so we had that in common. He had a son Kevin who also lived with us on the farm.'

'I'm sorry, but could you please tell me about the day of your stepson's death?'

'Sometimes I think I'm going crazy. It's like a record that never stops playing.' Rose gazed across the ocean. 'I remember I was stewing apricots. Isn't that a strange thing to remember? You know, I can't even smell an apricot now without the memories flooding back. Sorry, I'm jibber-jabbering.'

'No need to apologize. You are doing just fine. Take your time.'

'My husband Hank had taken the two boys camping at Sunny Ridge for the weekend.'

'How did you hear the news of the accident?' Sarah asked.

'There was a knock at the door, which was unusual because we rarely had visitors on the farm. I opened the door to see Sergeant Baxley looking at his feet. As he removed his hat I knew something terrible had happened. He said I needed to come down to the hospital as my stepson Kevin had suffered a terrible accident at Sunny Ridge. He said Kevin had fallen down a ravine and didn't survive. They said he must have been too close to the edge and slipped. I felt overwhelmed with relief it wasn't my son Luke, then a terrible feeling of dread for Hank. He adored his son.'

'Do you remember whose idea it was to go camping?' James asked.

'It was Luke's idea. I was surprised he'd asked.'

'Why were you surprised?'

'Luke generally hated camping and his relationship with his stepdad and Kevin was strained.'

James tilted his head to one side, a habit he had when something grabbed his attention. 'What do you mean by strained?'

'Luke and Kevin would occasionally have a punch-up, but I thought it was just normal fighting and it would take a while for them to adjust to living together as stepbrothers. There was one incident though. It seemed...mm...too ludicrous at the time.'

'The smallest amount of information can be the most important,' James said. 'What did you think was ludicrous?'

'Kevin found his cat stabbed to death in a back paddock. He blamed Luke for it.'

James and Sarah exchanged a knowing glance.

'He said Luke had threatened to kill his cat. He said Luke was crazy. I didn't believe him. I could not have imagined, in my wildest dreams, that my son could've been so cruel, and I certainly didn't think of him as being crazy. Having fist fights was one thing but killing his stepbrother's cat... That's not how I'd raised Luke.'

'Did you ask Luke about the incident?' James asked.

'I did,' Rose answered. 'He said he didn't do it and that it was Kevin trying to make him look bad. It was then, Luke said he wanted them to leave the farm, but I knew that was not possible. I loved Hank and besides, I couldn't run the property on my own. After Luke's father left, we had no money and we needed help. I didn't want to jeopardize my relationship, or lose the farm. I hadn't worked for ten years, and jobs were hard to find in a small country town.'

'Did Luke have any contact with his biological dad?' Sarah asked.

'He tried to call him numerous times, but his father didn't

want anything to do with him. The day he walked out on us, he didn't even leave a note.'

Sarah continued. 'How would you describe his relationship with his father?'

'Luke would spend hours in his room alone hoping his father would contact him. The rejection devastated him which surprised me.'

Now James was interested. 'Why did it surprise you?' asked James.

'His father was a former army soldier and was strict. If Luke didn't do his daily chores, he'd discipline him.'

James explored further. 'What was the discipline?'

'He'd have to hold a bucket of fruit on his head and run from the house to the property gates and back again several times followed by fifty push-ups. His father said it was character building and taught him grit. He called it his military program of perseverance and loyalty.'

James view of character building was having a father who provided unconditional love and support. Not a father who modelled aggression and the misuse of power. James resisted voicing his thoughts.

'When Luke's father proposed to me, he said he loved me and couldn't live without me. I realized his idea of marriage meant he could order us around.'

James continued. 'How old was Luke when his father left?'

'He was twelve. I woke up in the morning and his father was gone, along with all his belongings. I thought he would come back. Although I was relieved he'd gone, we were left to struggle on the farm. It was some months later I heard he'd met another woman. Luke and I continued to look after the farm until the day that Hank came with his son Kevin looking for a room and work. They never left. At the time, they were a Godsend.'

James continued his note taking during the questioning.

'Was there anything unusual you noticed about Luke during the time of his stepbrother's death?'

'Luke's behavior seemed odd.'

'What did you notice was odd?' James asked.

'When the wake had finished, and the guests had left, I walked past the dining room and noticed something.'

James didn't miss a beat and continued the flow of questions. 'What did you notice?'

'He was happily humming as if nothing had happened and eating the food the guests had left. I didn't think it was normal behavior. That same week I took him to a grief and loss counselor.'

James guessed Rose's concerns were valid. 'How did that go?' James asked.

'I told the counselor that my son's behavior didn't seem normal, that he was unusually happy on his stepbrother's funeral day. I was frank with the counselor, but it fell on deaf ears. The counselor said there was no such thing as normal and that children grieve differently from adults depending on how they make sense of their world. What she said is still a crystal-clear memory. She sounded educated but somewhat dismissive. Then I doubted myself.'

James sensitively continued. 'The police report stated your husband suicided a couple of weeks after his son's funeral, is that right?'

Rose slowly shook her head from side to side. 'I feel so guilty. I didn't see it coming. I didn't see any signs. I go over and over that week searching for clues. Searching for something that I might have missed.' Rose rotated her wedding ring. 'Suicides in the country are not uncommon, especially if the husband's life insurance can pay off the farm. But this wasn't the case. We had just paid off the mortgage, and the profits from the apple orchard were the best we'd ever had. The death of his son must have been too much for him to bear. I just wished he had talked to me. I wished I could have helped him cope.'

James knew they had her trust and he needed to dig further. 'Where was Luke when his stepdad took his life?'

'He'd told the police he was working in the back-paddock stacking crates and hadn't heard or seen anything.'

'Was anyone else on the property?' James asked.

'No. There was only Luke and his stepdad. The fruit pickers had finished at midday before I'd left for the markets.'

'Who'd discovered Hank?'

'I did. When I arrived home, I saw Hank's pickup truck at the front gates. I remember thinking how strange that was.'

'Why did you think that was strange,' James asked.

'He was always careful where he parked. The pickup was his pride and joy. Leaving the pickup at the front gates was something he wouldn't have done. There was so much blood. It still haunts me.'

James continued. 'Was there anything else you remember?'

'I remember Luke running towards me. He must have heard me screaming. I'm sorry, I can't remember any more. I couldn't understand why he'd killed himself. It just wasn't like him to take his own life.'

'What did the police tell you about the incident?' Sarah asked.

'The police said the keys were still in the ignition. They said Hank was so distressed over the death of his son he must have decided to kill himself there and then.'

James thought it made sense what the police had said, but he wasn't buying it. *Why hadn't Luke heard the gunshot, yet he'd heard his mum screaming? Why would Hank shoot himself in his pickup at the front gates and not elsewhere on the property? Had he been in a hurry? A desperate hurry to escape his killer?*

Sarah and James had read the police report. There had been a single bullet wound to the head. James glanced at Sarah. He knew that Luke had the opportunity, the means, and the motive to kill his stepdad. With the stepbrother and his step-dad eliminated, the farm would be Luke's and he would be the sole focus of his mom's attention.

James had worked on cases where kids had killed a family member, or their entire family. It was nothing new to him. He had seen it all. He also knew that child killers could go under the radar if the police were inexperienced with such young killers.

Rose was surprisingly blunt. 'Do you think Luke had anything to do with their deaths?'

Sarah and James looked at each. 'We're not sure what happened but we will certainly let you know if we need to talk to you again,' Sarah replied.

'Oh dear, what have I done,' Rose whispered.

Sarah could see her tears building and gave her a heartfelt response. 'We know this has been hard for you and we're sorry for your loss. Thank you for your time, Rose.'

'There's something I would like to ask you before you go, Lieutenant,' Rose said.

'Absolutely, and what would that be?' Sarah asked.

Rose gazed back at the ocean as she briefly reflected on the past. 'Do you think nature soothes the soul, Lieutenant?'

'Yes, I do. It clears the mind and warms the heart.'

'I knew you were a wise woman, Lieutenant. Do come again if you have any further questions.'

'I will. Here's my card. Call me anytime if you have any further information or remember anything else.' Sarah sensed visitors were rare for Rose, and so she found it difficult to walk away.

Sarah looked at James as they approached the chopper. 'Great questioning James. You haven't lost your touch.'

'I'm a bit rusty but once I get started, it all comes back. But now it's getting back to the paperwork. I can hardly wait.'

'Yeah, paperwork, it's absolutely riveting,' Sarah grinned.

THIRTY-SEVEN

ENTRAPMENT

Rose made her way back to her room with Nurse Lauren. Lauren had looked after her for three years and she was her closest companion. She had a tall slender figure and jet-black shoulder-length hair that fell in soft curls. She was half Rose's age, but they were more like close sisters.

'Is everything ok, Rose?' Lauren asked in a gentle voice.

'I would like to see my son Luke and I need your help,' Rose whispered.

'Anything Rose, you know I have a soft spot for you, what is it?'

'I'd always hoped I was wrong, but it's time to find out the truth about my son Luke. Do you remember Luke?'

'Of course,' responded Lauren. 'Dr Luke Ellison is a fine example of the nouveau riche in his expensive business suit and flash car. On his last visit, I noticed he was on his best behavior. He ate Mrs Maple's sandwiches while she slept and tucked her tissue packet in his pocket.'

Rose laughed. 'You don't miss a thing. We have a game to play with my darling, compassionate Luke. I'm not the fool he thinks I am. Are you up for it?'

Lauren's eyes sparkled. 'Oh Rose, I'm up for anything in this cold and dreary place.'

* * *

Meanwhile, the doctor was checking his bank account. His bank balance had almost doubled since the year before. The last delivery had been a street kid. He didn't often pick up the homeless, but she was a little stunner. There was a greater risk of being seen taking a kid off the streets, but he hadn't been able to resist the opportunity. He'd shown her pictures of his family and bought her dinner. His plan had worked without a glitch and he was proud of how well he had executed such a profitable catch.

Then he received the call he'd been waiting for. His boys had caught up with Curtis and were on his trail. Curtis would arrive just before sundown. If he didn't head for Brooklyn he trusted his boys to finish him off, but he'd be waiting at Curtis's apartment hoping he'd have the pleasure. This would give him enough time to see his favorite hooker and celebrate his latest financial windfall.

Her name was Lolly. She had blonde hair that fell to her waist, and her breasts were perky and round. She was no older than fifteen. She cost him a few thousand dollars, but it satisfied his twisted appetite. To kill her would cost him a lot more. One day he hoped to choke the life out of her tiny frame and watch the blood drain from her body but for now, he was content to play cat and mouse.

The sound of his cell disturbed his thirst for sex.

'Hello, Doctor Ellison speaking.'

'Hello Doctor, it's Lauren, your mom's nurse.'

'Why are you calling?' The doctor was more annoyed than alarmed. He didn't want his mom to get in the way of his sex games.

'I'm sorry to disturb you, Doctor, but we are concerned about your mom's dementia. We think she could have Alzheimer's.

It seems to be getting worse and we need to see you regarding her condition.'

'I understand that, but can't you just tell me over the phone?' he snapped.

'Sorry, Doctor, but we require your signature agreeing to your mom's change of medication, so she can start taking it tonight.'

The doctor's response was cold. 'Why can't this be done by your doctors. I pay big money for her to be in a retirement home and get the best care, so I don't have to be bothered with such trivia.'

'I'm sorry, Sir, I do understand but unfortunately I have to follow procedures.'

'Very well then, I will see you this afternoon. The quicker I get this done the better.'

The doctor ended the call. He was furious he couldn't have his young piece of ass to satisfy his appetite. He gritted his teeth with anger knowing he'd need to rush back to finish off Curtis.

He hoped his mom's Alzheimer's would provide a rapid decay of her neural connections, destroying her memory until she couldn't breathe. She was a nuisance. The last thing he wanted to do was to drive out to Long Island every time there was a problem. He was tired of acting like a caring son, especially as she was a financial liability. His thoughts switched to childhood memories of his mom. *You wasted your life on losers. Because of you I was unhappy. You didn't give a shit about me.*

Lauren finished the call and hurried back to Rose.

'How did my darling son respond?' Rose asked.

'He swallowed the story like a pelican with a fish. He was so considerate and sensitive to your needs. He has such a caring and kind nature and his empathy just overflowed,' Lauren laughed.

'Thank you, Lauren. Without your positivity, I know I'd already be six feet under.'

'You don't need to thank me. You know I would do anything for you, Rose.'

'I have something for you,' Rose stated. 'It was for Christmas, but I think this is the perfect time.'

She presented her nurse with a neat package.

Lauren unwrapped her gift. 'Oh Rose, I just love the colors. You shouldn't have.' She held up a pair of silk pajamas printed with delicate red and yellow wild flowers.

'I'm so glad you like the colors. Red means power and courage and yellow represents hope and happiness. A fitting present for you, don't you think Lauren?'

Lauren gave Rose a big hug.

Rose had seen residents spiral downward into dementia and die because of the pain of depression and loneliness so she felt blessed she had Lauren's friendship.

'Now Rose, what would you like to wear for your darling son? You have to look nice for such a special occasion.'

Their laughter reverberated down the hallway.

A nurse popped her head into the room. 'Please be quiet. There are residents sleeping.'

Rose and Lauren looked at each other and laughed even louder.

Rose raised her eyebrows. 'Now it's time for me to find out what really happened to my dear husband and stepson all that time ago.'

Lauren held Rose's hand. 'We'd better get a move on then. He's leaving Manhattan now.'

THIRTY-EIGHT

UNCONDITIONAL LOVE

The doctor pulled into the Kennedy Home and parked in a spot sign-posted 'Ambulances only'.

He stepped out of the car, hoping for a quick visit. He had to get back before Curtis arrived in Brooklyn. He pressed the security intercom at the main entrance. 'Hello, is anyone going to open these doors?'

A voice responded. 'Right away, Sir.' The double glass doors opened into the lobby.

He approached the desk clerk and announced himself, then admired the herringbone flooring and an antique chandelier hanging in the same place as it had a hundred years earlier. 'She lives in the most expensive retirement home on Long Island and I still have to do their fuckin' job,' he swore under his breath.

'Please take a seat, Doctor. I will call your mom's nurse now.'

'No, I'm not taking a seat. I need this matter to be dealt with quickly. I have important business to attend to.'

His petulance reminded the desk clerk of her five-year-old nephew.

'I've called the nurse, she will see you shortly, Doctor.'

A voice came from behind him. 'Hello Dr Ellison, how are you?'

'Enough of the small talk. You stated that I had to sign some papers. Can we make this quick?'

'Yes, of course, but first it's important I let you know some sad news. Your mom already has difficultly knowing where she is. She can have quite a lengthy discussion and then soon forgets the conversation. She is also losing facial recognition. We think it may have been due to her recent stroke.'

'Can I see the medical report?' the doctor asked.

Lauren produced the papers. She was as scared as hell. If she didn't pull this off, she risked losing her job. She had no choice but to fake her confidence and then lure him into his mom's room.

The doctor flicked through the physical and mental health assessment.

Lauren said, 'It's important you sign the documentation to authorize medication. I have the remaining forms in your mom's room. It may be a good idea to have as much quality time with your mom while you can.'

'What's the point of spending time with her if she's going to forget me anyway,' he said coldly.

'It may be the last time she will recognize you. She is going downhill fast. It may not be long before she is bedridden and needs total care.'

'This better not take long,' the doctor sighed. 'I will see her and sign these goddam documents. I can't understand why I pay big money to do your job.' *The bloody old nuisance*, he thought. He didn't care about her memory. He just wanted to get out of there.

Rose was sitting up in bed staring into space when they entered her room, seemingly in a catatonic state.

'Rose, I have a visitor for you. It's your son, Luke. He's come to see you.'

'Who has come to see me?'

'Your son, Luke. He's here for a visit.'

Rose smiled. 'Oh yes, Luke. How could I forget my only son?'

Little did the doctor know that his mom spoke with biting sarcasm.

'I will return soon.' Lauren left the room without waiting for his response. She paced the corridors as the minutes ticked by excruciatingly slowly.

He leaned over the bed and kissed Rose's forehead. 'Hello Mother. I brought you some chocolates.'

Rose found his voice nauseating.

'Sorry? Who are you?'

'I'm your son, Luke.'

'Oh yes, sorry Luke, I'm rather forgetful.'

'Here, I have a box of chocolates for you.'

'Thank you, Luke, you are so thoughtful. Are you still working as a psychologist?'

'Of course, helping people is what I do best. How is your health, Mother?'

'I'm a bit confused lately. Where am I? Why do I have nurses looking after me? Can I come home with you?'

'Mother, you're at the Kennedy Nursing Home on Long Island. It's important you stay here for the best possible treatment and care.'

'Luke, I keep having these nightmares. I dreamed you did a terrible thing when you were a young boy.'

Her son came closer to the bed. 'What are these nightmares, Mother?'

'I had a dream that you hurt your stepbrother Kevin. Tell me it isn't true, Luke.'

His stare was chilling. Did he suspect her plan of entrapment?

'Your dreams are truly disturbing, Mother. Do you think I killed my stepbrother?'

'I don't know, Luke.'

He gave her an evil grin. 'What if I told you the truth?'

'I love you and nothing you could say or do would change that. You are my sweet boy and the only person on this earth who cares about me. I will always stand by you no matter what.'

Luke stepped closer. Rose could now smell his breath. 'I killed him and in fact, my stepfather as well. Did you really expect me to put up with their arrogant presence? They treated me like shit. I deserved better.'

Rose's gaze wandered, as if she hadn't really heard him.

He continued. 'You married such a loser and you gave me no choice but to eliminate them. They were out to destroy us and take the farm. We would have been left with nothing.'

Rose felt sick to her stomach, but she didn't flinch. She couldn't believe she had given birth to a monster who justified his evil. She realized he had no conscience. She knew she had to continue the pretense to entrap him.

Rose gazed at him, 'I am so sorry I ruined your childhood Luke. It must have been dreadful for you. I hope you can forgive me. I just have one question though, how did you kill your stepbrother?'

'It was easy. I planned the camping trip. You really think I wanted to spend time with those fuckin' assholes? I played the role of the good child. It only took one push and he bounced off the rocks like a rag doll. As for my stepdad, he was an imbecile to think I was going to put up with him. He tried to get away, but he only made it to the gates. You should have seen his face. I shot him at point blank range. He cried like a baby and begged for mercy. He was pathetic.'

Rose remembered the headlines: *Terrible accident...camping trip...leads to suicide of traumatized father. Loss of son too much to bear.* She hoped he couldn't hear her pounding heart and see the revulsion in her eyes.

He placed his hand on hers and leaned slowly across the bed.

Her stomach lurched when she felt his touch.

'You see, Mother dearest, I did it for us.'

The doctor stood up as Lauren entered the room.

Rose was relieved to see her.

'How did you go with the forms, Doctor?'

'I'm signing them now.'

Rose turned to look at Lauren. 'Do I know you?'

'I'm Lauren, your nurse.' Lauren approached the bed as if to reassure Rose. 'It's ok, Rose. I'm going to give you some medication that will help you sleep.'

Rose looked bewildered. 'Who is this man in my room?'

'It's Luke, your son. He came for a visit.'

'Oh dear. I'm so forgetful. I can't even remember my own son.'

Lauren looked at the doctor meaningfully. 'Thank you for signing the forms. As you can see, it's important she start this medication as soon as possible. I'm so sorry, but she won't be able to remember your visit. Unfortunately, Doctor, as you would know, Alzheimer's is such a debilitating disease, not only for the patient but for family and friends.'

'Yes, I'm well aware of that. They call it the walking dead,' the doctor quipped.

'If you need any further information, let me know,' Lauren responded, trying to keep her voice level.

'I need to get out of here. As far as I'm concerned you've already wasted enough of my time.'

Rose closed her eyes, pretending to drift off to sleep. She could not bear to look at him. She knew he was not only evil but dangerous.

The doctor turned to kiss his mother goodbye but then pulled back. 'I must be off. Say goodbye to my mother when she wakes, that is, if she remembers me.' He couldn't believe his luck. His mom was losing her memory and soon, the memories of his childhood would be dead with her. He congratulated himself on committing the perfect crime. Before leaving the room, he snatched back his gift of chocolates. *No sense wasting them when she won't even remember me being here,* he thought.

Rose was relieved not to feel the touch of his lips. She kept her eyes closed, hoping her eyelids weren't flickering, and continued to breathe deeply.

'I will see you out, thanks so much for coming.' *You black-hearted mongrel,* Lauren thought. She did not expect him to reply. She let him out through the front doors and watched his vehicle screech away.

Ten minutes into the drive to Brooklyn, his eyes narrowed, and his thoughts turned to nurse Lauren. He had spoken with the nurse before but this time he'd noticed something different about her demeanor. Her speech had been rapid, and she'd seemed anxious. He eased his foot off the accelerator. He also thought of his mother being extremely lucid and communicative, then suddenly quite vague. Something didn't fit. As the vehicle slowed, he pulled off the road. He sat in silence with both hands still on the wheel, wondering whether to go back. He was pushed for time. He knew if he returned to the nursing home he would have to be quick.

He looked at his mom's box of chocolates on the passenger seat and ripped open the lid to scoop up a chocolate-coated caramel. His favorite. *What a good idea,* he thought as he delicately rolled the chocolate around his tongue.

The flavor of his favorite chocolate was enough to distract him. His thoughts switched to the other thing he had a taste for: murder. His eye twitched with the memory of his stepbrother screaming with terror as he bounced off the ravine's jagged edge. His body landing on the canyon floor. The force of the impact caused cerebrospinal fluid to spill from his cracked skull and ooze through his nose. He imagined with delight, the thickness and volume of his stepbrother's blood. The funeral had gone off without a glitch. He had played the role of a grieving stepbrother. He was surprised at how easily he'd been able to carry out his plan and fool everyone. It was then he learned how satisfying it was to manipulate others to meet his needs.

His smartwatch buzzed. A message confirmed that Curtis was still alive and heading towards the city. He hoped it was Brooklyn. The Doctor continued his journey, enjoying the thought of finishing him off.

THIRTY-NINE

SYMBIOTIC RELATIONSHIP

After ten minutes, Lauren hurried back to Rose. 'Sorry I kept you waiting, Rose. I wanted to make sure he was definitely gone.'

Rose sat up. 'Thank you, Lauren. For a moment, I thought he was onto us. I think it's time I called Lieutenant Wilkins.'

Rose was trying to remain detached from the horror of what her son had admitted. It wasn't the time to cry but to stay focused until the Lieutenant had the cell phone. The cell Lauren had set up in video mode in a display of flowers opposite her bed. She had to get it to the NYPD as quickly as possible.

Rose dialed the NYPD number. 'Hello, can I speak to Lieutenant Wilkins please. She'd asked me to call her if I had any further information.'

'Certainly, I'll transfer you,' responded the desk clerk.

'Lieutenant Wilkins speaking.'

'Hello Lieutenant, it's Rose Ellison. You came to see me this morning.'

'Yes, that's right, how can I help you Rose?'

'I have just seen my son and I have something for you. Evidence on a cell video recording that proves he is a killer. How quickly can you get here?'

Sarah hastily grabbed a notebook and pen, nearly knocking

over her coffee. 'Rose, it's really important that I have heard you correctly.' Sarah spoke with clear intention. 'Did you just tell me that you have a video recording that proves your son is a killer, is that correct?'

'Yes, that's right. He admitted killing my husband and his stepbrother. Lauren, my nurse, hid her cell phone in a vase of flowers opposite my bed.'

'An officer will leave straightaway to collect the evidence. Thank you, Rose. I understand how hard this must be for you.'

'I don't have a choice. To say nothing would make me equally evil,' Rose replied.

'Before you go, Rose, can I have a quick word with Nurse Lauren?' Sarah asked.

'Absolutely, I will put her on.'

'Lauren speaking.'

'Hello Lauren. This is Lieutenant Wilkins. Could you please alert your security to keep all doors and windows locked and not to allow anyone in. I mean no one at all! Unfortunately, I will need your cell for evidence, but I will make sure you get it back as soon as possible.'

'I'm in no rush to get it back. I have another cell. That was a spare,' Lauren responded.

'I will contact the local police to secure the building until our team arrive. I don't want the doctor suspecting something and returning. Please do not tell anyone what is happening. Do you understand?'

'Yes, absolutely.' Lauren ended the call.

Rose felt breathless with self-doubt. 'I raised my son so he would be a good man. Did I create that monster, Lauren? Was there something I should have done differently? Where did I go wrong?'

'Don't own his evil, Rose, you were a good mom. You faced the truth. He could have easily killed you. The quicker we get this evidence to the police the better.'

'Oh Lauren, thank you for letting the police have your cell.'

'Keeping a spare cell paid off. The main thing is that you are safe,' Lauren Responded.

Lauren gave Rose a gentle hug and then secured the building.

* * *

Sarah prepared all the necessary documents for the doctor's arrest while she waited for the chopper to return with the cell. She wasn't going to relax until it was in her hands.

Unexpectedly, her office door swung open and Mick, a cop from her team, peered in. 'Sorry to interrupt, Lieutenant, but we have a guy from Vegas on the phone. His name is Mohsen. He said he's an imam in Vegas and he knows of a boy who may have been abducted from Manhattan and is being held captive by a pastor. The call was put through by an ex-colleague of yours, McQueen at the Central Park Precinct.'

Sarah was swamped with paperwork and didn't look up. 'Why the hell would this imam call New York? And why are you bothering me about this? I'm under the gun here! It sounds urgent. Give him the number of the Vegas Police Department, for God's sake.' Sarah continued to flick through her case notes.

Mick gave a slight cough as if mustering up enough courage to continue. 'There may be a connection with the commissioner's niece and what this imam is saying.'

'What are you talking about Mick?'

'Wasn't one of the victims Linda Maloney?'

'Yes! The commissioner's niece,' Sarah snapped.

'Her body was found at Lake Mead in Boulder City. There could be a connection between the commissioner's niece found at Lake Mead and this boy whose being held captive in Vegas,' Mick answered. 'It sounds like a long shot, but this boy could be the pedestrian who was pulled into the van on 5th Avenue.'

'Hell yes, that's right! Great work, Mick. You're a genius.

Put the imam through. There is one other thing Mick. When a package from Long Island arrives, bring it straight to me.'

'Will do,' he responded.

'James!' Sarah called. 'Come in here quickly. I want you to listen to this.'

Sarah waited for the transfer then pressed speakerphone.

'Hello, Lieutenant Wilkins speaking, can I help you?'

'I'm sorry to disturb you, Lieutenant, but I called the Central Park Precinct and they put the call through to you.'

'You're not disturbing me at all. I understand you have some information you would like to report?'

'My name is Mohsen and I'm risking my family's life making this call. I must be quick. I don't know if my cell is being tapped.'

'I'm listening, Mohsen.'

'There's a pastor in Vegas. His name is pastor Sleeman. He's the founder of the Vegas Savior's Church. He's doing bad things to people and he may be keeping a boy captive. The boy's name is Sean Young and as far as I know, he was abducted from Manhattan.'

'How do you know all this?'

'I help the homeless and I work at a soup kitchen. I hear lots of things.'

'Why haven't you reported this to the Vegas police?'

'It wouldn't be safe. What's going on around the world isn't good for a Muslim and from what I've been told, pastor Sleeman knows lots of people in high places who get paid hush money.'

'Do you know where this pastor lives?'

'No, but the police would. He has two places just out of Vegas. His family lives in one and he calls the other place The Lord's House of Therapy. I've been told he's keeping this boy at the Therapy House.'

'Have you told anyone?' Sarah asked.

'No one. Not even my family.'

'Do not talk to anyone about this. Thank you, Mohsen. You are a man of moral courage. I know this is dangerous for you. I'm on my way but you must promise not to tell a soul.'

'If I told anyone, I know my family would not be safe,' Mohsen whispered.

'Can I contact you on this number if I need to?' Sarah asked.

'Yes.'

'You will be hearing from me again, Mohsen.'

Sarah ended the call and tossed the paperwork to one side. 'What do you make of it, James?'

'Our psychologist Doctor Ellison is not a lone wolf. Sounds like he could be making donations to a Vegas pastor, and I don't mean financial donations. These ones are alive and kicking. It would explain why he's been under the radar for so long and why the clients vanish. This could be the kid that was pulled into the van on 5th Avenue.'

Sarah's heart raced. 'He has a courier service that operates from New York and deals with live deliveries! It would make sense why the commissioner's niece was found at Lake Mead.'

'Exactly,' James said. 'This psych outsourced his clients to a killer. I'm predicting the killer is our pastor and he's the accomplice who lost his glasses on his murderous dumping ground at Lake Mead.'

Sarah visualized the pastor like a storm cloud looming over Vegas. 'I'll let the commissioner know what's going down. He can make up some story about a diplomat visiting Vegas and that we need the NYPD there for emergency surveillance of the area for security reasons. If there's a snitch in the Vegas Police Department and the pastor finds out he's a suspect, then our pastor may do a runner or get rid of any evidence.'

Sarah counted the minutes. Getting evidence from Long Island seemed to take forever. She was relieved when Mick returned.

'Here's your parcel from Long Island.'

'Great job, Mick. I'm shouting you a dinner this Friday night and a few beers! You may have just cracked this case right open. Don't tell anyone about our Vegas visit. If word gets out, then our suspects could get spooked and disappear. The quicker we get to this pastor in Vegas without him knowing, the better the chance of getting two killers and wrapping up this case.'

'Sorry for the short notice James, but how do you feel about flying in the commissioner's jet to visit Vegas?'

'A trip to Vegas in a jet? I wouldn't miss it for the world, especially if I'm going to witness the arrest of a wolf in sheep's clothing.'

FORTY

THE POISONED DWARF

Magda Sleeman was travelling home after shopping for some light snacks for the Book Club Meetup that was going to be held at her place, when she suddenly realized she had forgotten to buy coffee. Rather than turn back, she decided to call her husband and ask him to buy a jar on his way home.

'Hello, it's Mrs Sleeman speaking, may I speak to my husband?'

'I'm sorry Mrs Sleeman, he has already left.'

'Oh ok. That's odd. I thought he was going to be at the Church until 5.00 pm.'

'He may be at The Lord's House of Therapy.'

Magda rang her husband and wasn't surprised when it went to message bank.

She knew where The Lord's House of Therapy was located. No one was allowed there, as it was for parishioners who wished for privacy while receiving spiritual healing. She looked at Helga playing with her doll in the front seat of the vehicle and bit her lower lip, then turned the wheel in the direction of Krampus Street, the street that was out of bounds. Her heart began to race but she reassured herself there was no harm in having a look as she parked the car.

'Why aren't we going home? Why have we parked here, Mommy?' Helga asked.

'I'm just here to see Daddy.'

'Oh goodie!' Helga squealed.

'Helga, you stay here. I won't be long.'

'That's not fair, I want to come. Please, please! I want to see Daddy.'

'Ok, but stay close behind me and don't make a noise. Be as quiet as a mouse, like you are at church.'

As Magda approached the property, a van was coming out through the security gates. She grabbed Helga's hand and ducked for cover.

'This is so exciting!' Helga shouted.

'Shoosh. You'll go back to the vehicle if you're not quiet.'

Once the van disappeared, Magda walked towards the house. She could hear a young girl crying. She slipped inside the house gates. *Why am I being so foolish?* she wondered. It was unlike her to take risks. She wanted to leave but now, it was too late. The gates closed behind her.

'Hello Magda, what brings you here?' It was her husband's voice.

Magda jumped. After a moment's pause, she caught her breath. 'Hello Joseph, how did you know I was here?'

Joseph smirked. 'CCTV is useful. You don't know who could be lurking around these corners.'

'Hello Daddy, Mommy said we could see you.'

'Did she now? Funny that.' Sleeman gave his wife a piercing stare. 'I thought you knew The Lord's House of Therapy was off limits. My parishioners need their privacy.'

Magda was good at massaging his ego. 'I forgot to buy coffee for The Book Club Meetup tonight and I thought you might have a jar here. Besides, I couldn't resist seeing the amazing work you do for those less fortunate. But of course, I wouldn't want to intrude on personal therapy and the meetup group arrive at 6.00 pm so I better get going.'

Joseph shook his head as he tsk-tsked. 'I will have no such thing. Come on in and I will get you some coffee, and then you must be off.'

'Ok darling, if you insist.'

'Daddy, I heard a girl crying. Who is she?'

'She is a girl who is crying for forgiveness. She has been a bad girl and needs to be punished. The Lord is helping her. She is asking for his help. It's all part of God's therapy.'

'What is wrong with her, Daddy?'

'She needs spiritual healing. You see darling, we must have parishioners cleansed of sin and impure thoughts if they want to enter the gates of heaven. They are lost souls and will be worthless to society if they are not healed.'

Suddenly Magda felt queasy. She wasn't sure whether it was her husband's words or his demeanor that frightened her.

Helga sensed her mom's fear and her father's different behavior. She stepped closer to her mom.

* * *

Little did the pastor know that the commissioner's jet had landed at McCarran Airport and the police would be at his property within minutes.

There was a Vegas cop waiting for them as soon as they disembarked from the plane. Sarah wondered how many cops were getting paid off by this pastor.

'Hello. I'm Lieutenant Wilkins and this is Detective Christianson.'

'Please to meet you. I'm Officer Eastwood. I've been told to take you to pastor Sleeman's home.'

'Yes, that's right. We need to go to The Lord's House of Therapy.'

The cop looked perplexed. 'Ok...but why The Lord's House

of Therapy? He has a home address. I can take you there.'

'Yes, we realize that, but it's important we are taken to the Therapy House.'

'The Therapy House it is.'

As the cop drove them from the airport, Sarah noticed his dark beady eyes squinting at her in his rear-vision mirror.

'What's so important that you need to see the pastor?'

'A diplomat from Manhattan will be visiting Vegas and we will be discussing security matters. Unfortunately, that's all I can tell you. It's highly classified.'

'Yeah, I understand. I understand totally,' the cop replied.

James considered himself a good judge of character, but he wasn't sure whether this cop was being genuine or sarcastic.

After only a few minutes on the road, the cop veered into a gas station.

'Why are we stopping here?' Sarah asked.

'Sorry, Lieutenant. I need some gas. We don't want to be stranded, do we?' he replied.

Sarah inconspicuously took a quick glance at the gas level. From what she could see, the tank was nowhere near empty. As he filled the tank, Sarah whispered to James without moving her lips, 'James, can you see how much gas this guy is pumping?'

'I can try.' James moved slightly forward, careful not to move his head, and glanced sideways.

'He's filled up ten dollars. Why would he need to fill the tank when it's almost full? The pastor's Therapy House is only fifteen minutes away.'

'Exactly,' Sarah whispered.

As the cop walked into the gas station, Sarah yelled, 'Let's move!'

They charged in through the station doors, but it was too late, he was on his cell.

'Freeze! Put your hands up!' Sarah screamed.

The cop dropped his cell.

'Well, what have we here. Let me guess. You were having a nice chat with your friend pastor Sleeman. Would that be right, Officer?' James asked.

Sarah couldn't believe it. Not five minutes on Vegas soil and she was handcuffing a cop. Now she understood the imam's fear.

Sarah shoved the cop towards his patrol car. 'Now, Officer Eastwood. You're going to be really smart and direct us to The Lord's House of Therapy, unless you would rather spend the rest of your life in the pen for being an accessory to multiple murders.'

FORTY-ONE

WOLF'S LAIR

Pastor Sleeman ended his call, having received the tip-off. The police were on their way. He knew it was over. He knew it was pointless to run. To him the solution was death and that meant taking Magda and Helga with him. He believed his followers and Magda had reported him. He was seething, furious that they had lied and betrayed him. *I will show the world. They will never forget me.*

'Who was that, darling?' Magda asked.

'It's nothing. Just another follower looking for spiritual guidance. Come now and let's get that coffee.'

Once they were in the house, he led them down a staircase. 'Come along, Helga. Come down the stairs.'

The stairway led to a basement.

His shorter leg and club foot was noticeable as he side-stepped down.

'Why are we going down here, Daddy? It looks creepy. Do you keep the coffee here?'

Joseph didn't answer.

As they stepped inside the basement, they saw gold candles glowing from niches within reinforced concrete walls, and a bed positioned in the corner.

'Why do you have candles, Joseph?' Magda asked.

'It removes evil toxins from the atmosphere and helps with spiritual healing.'

As they entered the room, Helga pointed to the wall. 'What's that, Daddy? What's that flag on the wall?'

Magda followed the direction of her daughter's finger. She froze with horror and disbelief. Draped across the wall was an equilateral cross with the emblem of an eagle.

'Joseph, this is a Nazi emblem.'

'Very clever, my darling Magda. You do know some history. Why do you think I changed your name to Magda? Joseph Goebbels and his wife Magda are my heroes of World War II.'

'I don't understand Joseph. What are you doing?' Magda responded.

'I am the Unit Leader for the National Socialist Party in Nevada. You see Magda, our destiny is a matter of choice and this is what I've chosen for us.'

'But Joseph, you are not German, and you have a disability. Hitler would've gassed you in the war.'

Joseph winced. 'I am the chosen one and I don't expect you to understand. We need to stay strong against the forces who go against our values and beliefs.'

Helga looked at her mom for reassurance and squeezed her hand. 'Mommy, I want to go home. Can we go now?'

'Not yet, my precious one.' Joseph stroked her plait.

'Mommy, I want to go home. I'm scared.'

'There, there. You stay here until I get you both a drink that tastes yummy and will help you to relax.'

The pastor climbed back up the basement stairs, where he wasted no time in getting the drinks and concealing a gun in his jacket.

Magda looked across the room. There was no escape.

'Mommy, Daddy's scaring me. I want to go. This place is creepy, even the candles are spooky.'

Suddenly from the darkness, they heard a voice. 'Please

help me. Please, he is going to kill me.'

Magda could see a section of the room concealed by a drape. She slowly edged forward until her fingers touched it and as she pulled it aside, she saw a sickening sight. A naked boy was suspended by his arms from the ceiling.

'My name is Sean. I'm from Manhattan. Please help me.'

Helga's mouth opened with shock, her innocent eyes staring in disbelief.

Magda looked at Sean and pressed her finger to her lips. 'You must be quiet. I will help you.'

Magda bent down and whispered to Helga, 'Helga, you have to do the most important thing of your life. You must be brave. We are going to play a pretend game. Remember that game we play and you're the super hero?'

'Yes, Mommy.'

'You are going to be that super hero like the character in your book. Do you understand?'

Helga knew exactly what her mom meant. 'Yes. I understand.'

Sean pointed to a hook on the wall where a key was suspended. In seconds, Magda grabbed the key and unlocked Sean from his chains, then she scanned the room. She could see there was no way out but back up the stairs.

'Mommy, Daddy's coming back.'

Sean cowered behind Magda's legs, his fear so overwhelming that he was shaking involuntarily. Malnourished and exhausted, he mumbled a prayer.

Joseph quietly shut the basement door, slid the bolt into place, and descended the stairs. Once he entered the basement room, he noticed the open drape. His toy was no longer suspended but crouched behind Magda. His suspicions were confirmed. Magda was out to destroy him.

He turned to his wife. 'So, Magda, I see you have met my other guest. The more the merrier, that's what I say.' He placed the drinks on a side table and pulled out his pistol.

Helga trembled by her mom's side. She had to pretend to be brave.

The pastor heard the voice of a young girl behind him. He swung around. 'Who are you? How did you get in here?' It wasn't possible that someone else had entered the basement.

Magda and Helga were bewildered. He was talking to someone who wasn't there, like a madman.

'Don't you recognize me?' Joseph heard the young girl say to him. 'Come closer. Take a good look.'

'Why would I recognize a scrawny, pale child?' Joseph aimed his pistol at her and waved it back and forth. 'Get over there with the others, now!' he yelled.

'Mommy, there's no one there. Who is Daddy talking to?'

Magda shook her head to silence Helga.

'I can see you still don't know who I am,' she said.

He thought her face was familiar. His demonic eyes fixed on the girl as he raised his gun and fired. The bullet passed right through her, ricocheted off the wall, and penetrated his leg.

In his psychotic rage, he frothed at the mouth and desperately hurled the drink tray at her. It too passed through her, hitting several candles off a shelf. The candles landed on the bed and within seconds, the bedding was alight. Smoke began filling the room.

Helga yelled. 'Mommy, Mommy, everything is burning!'

Magda grabbed Sean's and her daughter's hands and they scrambled up the stairs. Helga listened to her father's ranting all the way until they reached the top of the stairway. Once at the top, Magda desperately pulled the bolt back and opened the door. They could hear a police siren.

Joseph was on the ground aiming the gun up the stairway.

'Joseph, you must remember me. I am Anne Frank. I'm surprised you don't remember me, especially as you love to wallow in past atrocities.'

His attention flicked back to the vision and his expression changed from arrogance to confusion.

'You remember me now, don't you? I'm sure of all people, you would recognize me. I was dead and now I am alive.'

'You're tricking me! You are not real!' he screamed. 'You cannot be Anne Frank; you are dead. You are all traitors.'

Filled with rage, Joseph shrieked, 'My people have betrayed me! They're all liars! They are nothing but garbage.'

The vision spoke to him calmly. 'You blame others for your physical imperfections and childhood rejection. It is sad to think you did not find beauty in this world and became an evil monster who vomits hate speech. It is now up to you to find any goodness within you. How you end this lies in your own hands.'

Dissociated from reality, Joseph stumbled towards Anne, shaking and with spittle forming on his lips, blinded by his lust for control. His hands reached out to grip her neck but there was no one there.

Flames were now licking the Nazi flag.

Joseph stood upright facing the black and white eagle. He raised his arm in a Nazi salute as he held the pistol in his left hand.

'Heil, Mein Fuhrer!' he yelled.

He aimed the pistol to his left temple and pressed the trigger.

In his haste, he had fired the bullet through his left eye socket and it had exited through the right side of his skull. Blood splatter decorated the eagle as he fell to the floor.

FORTY-TWO

A MEANS TO AN END

Red dropped me off on Lewis. 'Thanks, Red. I'll let you know what happens. I owe you big time.'

'Shoot that motherfucker in the balls. Animal would love that.'

'With pleasure,' I replied.

Red took off with a wave.

I looked and felt like shit. I needed a quick shower and then it was payback time. Once at my apartment door I wondered how I was going to get in without my keys. Then I thought of the external stairs but before I could turn around, I heard a familiar voice.

'Hello, Curtis.'

I froze. Shit! *Now I'm truly fucked.* I had no energy to run. I was sure I'd watched my back. Obviously a fuckin' skilled predator.

'Don't turn around or you're a dead man. You really think you could outsmart a psychologist? You think you can come here and take everything away from me? Now put the gun and your cell on the ground!'

I reluctantly squatted down and placed them by my feet.

'The problem with you, Curtis, is you're a small-time loser. Now, let me tell you what's going to happen. We're going to walk out of here and then go for a little walk up Lewis. Any sudden movement and you're dead, hear me? I would just be the innocent victim, defending myself. You don't get it, Curtis. But don't feel bad. Most people like you are just plain stupid. Because of that, I have a bank account with enough money to do anything I want. Now start walking!'

Fuckin' bastard, I thought. 'You're not a psychologist. You're a thug. Your PhD gave you a license to kill. You hide behind your fancy words when you're nothing but a depraved killer. A fuckin' monster. The police are looking for me. You haven't got a chance in getting away with this.'

It couldn't end here. I prayed I was being watched by hidden surveillance.

'Move. Keep walking and don't turn around.'

Step by step I was being directed out of the apartment block and along Lewis.

'Turn right, Curtis, we don't want anyone seeing us now, do we.'

Turning right meant being in a darkened alleyway hidden from the streets. I didn't believe in God until I felt a gun on my neck. I prayed to Jesus and Allah, hoping two was better than one.

'You're a fuckin' deviant, a murderer.'

'Killing you will relieve my tension. That makes deviance socially functional don't you think?'

'Go to hell, you motherfucker!'

'Shut up and keep moving.'

I continued down the alleyway until I was facing a brick wall. I was desperate to keep him talking. 'The police know everything. It won't be long before they're here.'

'That's laughable, Curtis. In fact, you're funny. You continue to recycle your life, drifting from one job to another and getting nowhere, resulting in maladaptive outcomes. Your capacity development is...mm...let me see...innately limited. That means you're a catastrophic failure. An imbecile who has abnormal brain connections. That's why your visual and auditory skills are somewhat defunct. You came into this world as nothing and you'll leave it as nothing. Your life is meaningless. It won't be long before I'll put you out of your misery.'

'If you kill me you'll end up pissing in a jail cell.'

The doctor gave a sadistic smile and stepped closer. 'In case you don't know, Curtis, a dead man doesn't talk. Besides, I'm very well known in New York. I'm the one who's going to be the hero for killing a criminal. I write articles for the Psychological Society. I'm in the helping industry, Curtis. Do you know what that means? It means that people trust me. I'm also on the New York Ethical Review Board and assist in disciplinary matters of professional misconduct. Think about it, Curtis. You've lost, now turn around. I want to see the fear in your eyes. I want to see how brave you really are.'

'You're a deranged asshole!' I spat.

'Did your parents say they were proud of you? I'll tell you the truth, Curtis. They abandoned you emotionally. They rejected you because you're a goddam failure. In fact, your life is a dead end. Just like this alleyway. You've achieved nothing. You had this delusional ideal of being the hero, but your actual self is the loser. Funny that. This discrepancy must be quite traumatic for you Curtis. You see, my historical hero, Alfred Hoch, would classify you as a mental defect. Someone worthless who wouldn't be missed. This means, I can destroy you.'

I had nothing to lose. I had to go out with a fight. I jumped for the gun. It was enough to force it from his hands. It landed out of his reach.

Suddenly I was immobilized. I saw his evil sneer and a twitch in his cheek. I didn't understand. *Why was I standing still, unresisting?* I felt a cold sensation.

I instinctively gripped my stomach. It was wet, and I looked down at my bloodied fingers. The gun had been a diversion.

He had plunged a knife in my side. There was no struggle. My legs buckled.

'Well, well, well, Curtis, you failed to notice the obvious. You're not only inattentively blind, your capacity to evaluate danger is also severely impaired. Obviously, you're not the sharpest tool in the shed,' the doctor stated with a sardonic smirk. 'If all the losers in the world were put together, you'd be the shining example. You're the perfect prototype of a loser. Being a loser has one payoff. The last thing you will hear and see before leaving this world will be me. Such a soul inspiring way to die, don't you think? Die a slow death, Curtis, and don't take it to heart, you were just a means to an end.'

I slid down the wall until I was on the ground. I slumped sideways and cradled my stomach. He was holding the bloodied knife, his eyes cold and detached. The bastard had won. I was done.

Maybe he was right. Maybe my parents weren't proud of me and I deserve this.

Death by a dumpster was not what I'd imagined, but my will was fading.

FORTY-THREE

IF ONLY

The vagrant averaged two hours' sleep at a time. He was cradling his bottle like a baby, hoping that tonight the drink would numb his pain. Every second of every day he relived the horror. Overwhelming guilt was his constant companion. His nightmares left him shaking and breathless.

It had been two years since his life had changed in a burning flash. He had been driving his family to Montauk for the weekend when another driver, high on drugs, crashed into his vehicle with such force that his wife, son, and daughter were killed. Miraculously, he survived the accident along with the family dog Molly. His only physical scars were third-degree burns to his hands but when hospital staff said he was lucky to be alive, it only deepened his trauma.

He mumbled the same words every night as he stared at his scarred hands. 'Why did I insist on a family outing. If only I'd seen the vehicle coming. Why couldn't I take their place? I deserve to live among the trash.' The week after the accident he'd walked away from his triple-figure job and his extended family to set up home in the alley.

The vagrant was settling in for the night when he saw two men enter the alley. Living in the alley meant constant danger. Molly curled up on his lap as he squeezed further into a crevice and covered himself with cardboard. The voices of the men echoed along the alleyway walls. Something made him freeze. He recognized one of the voices. It was the voice that had saved Molly. The Good Samaritan. The other voice was menacing.

He wondered whether the bottle was making him hear voices. Now, they were telling him to help the Samaritan. In his mind, he argued back. *I couldn't help my family so how can I help anyone else. I need to be here for Molly.*

He argued with himself until he finally stood upright and tucked Molly out of sight. He quietly left the alleyway and hurried to a local cabbie who was having a smoko break on the sidewalk. He begged the cabbie to call police and then hurried back to the alley. He stood still to catch his breath, then ran both hands along the brick wall as he edged closer and closer to the sound of the voice. He held his breath, fearing he would be heard. He peeped carefully around the corner.

He could see a tall man wearing a suit. His black patent shoes were a sharp contrast to the surrounding gloom. The man's voice was smug.

'I forgot to tell you Curtis. I wasn't always a psychologist. I was once a prison guard. People looked up to me and fuckin' jumped when they knew I meant business. You see Curtis, to put it succinctly, behavior can be extinguished according to my rules. It's all about punishment being swift and certain. Certain meaning death if necessary. Today is different though, I'm in no rush. I'm enjoying the moment.'

The vagrant could see a small hand pistol on the ground. He hated guns and believed they were for cowards.

A demanding voice in his head pushed the vagrant to act. *'You've got to get to the gun. You have no choice. The Good Samaritan needs your help.'*

The vagrant moved towards the gun. He didn't want to

kill anyone. He noticed the Samaritan was on the ground and clutching his stomach. He was leaning forward, and his head was tilted to one side. Blood soaked his shirt.

FORTY-FOUR

THE HUMAN SPIRIT

I saw shadows. I wondered whether they were the shadows of the doctor's victims or if I was hallucinating.

I noticed another shadow, but it was unlike the others. It was taller. *Was this Death, or was I already dead?* The shadow gently picked up the gun, his hands shaking. I realized it was the vagrant who lived in the alleyway.

The doctor spun around, holding the bloodied knife.

I could see the vagrant's frightened expression. His hands were wobbling so much I was sure he would drop the gun.

'You...you...stand still until the police arrive. They're...they're...they're on their way,' the vagrant stammered.

The doctor decided he couldn't be defeated. 'I'm here to help. I'm protecting you from evil. See this man? He is evil, he's lost his mind. Trust me.'

I knew if the vagrant dropped the gun, it would be over. He would join me in the dumpster. Would he shoot? If he did, would his shaking hands make him miss the doctor?

'You say he's evil but you're the one with blood on your hands. You're the one holding the knife. I'll let the police work it out. You stay right there.'

I noticed the doctor stepping closer to the vagrant.

'You're imagining this. Give me the gun. My name is Dr

Ellison. I am a well-known psychologist in Manhattan. Your stress is hijacking your emotional state and your intrusive thoughts are impairing your capacity to make sense of this. You're acting irrationally. The alcohol has poisoned your brain and you have a distorted sense of reality. I'm not the bad guy. This man here. He is evil. He is the one you should be pointing the gun at. If you give me the gun, I will help you. I am a doctor. I can help free you of your addiction and your demons. Trust me.'

'I just drink too much! You're the demon. My hands shake but that doesn't mean I'm imagining this. I know exactly what I'm seeing.'

The doctor lunged towards the vagrant.

The vagrant pulled the trigger. I heard the gun discharge. The doctor stood in disbelief, gazing downwards. He slowly landed on his knees, as if praying to an evil power. He looked angered by his own demise. He pointed his bloodied finger at the vagrant in a desperate last attempt to exert his control.

'You're a loser. A bum on the street. You're nothing but a waste of space on this earth.'

The vagrant stood taller.

With blood trickling from the doctor's mouth, he fell face down. As he lay in a crumpled heap, the wind swirled around him.

With great relief, I felt my head being cradled.

'Help's on the way.'

My 'thank you' was merely a groan. I knew I'd lost a lot of blood, but the sound of sirens strengthened my will.

FORTY-FIVE

WISE WORDS

I woke to see a nurse standing at the end of my bed holding a clipboard. She was easily sixty and she had a 'don't mess with me' expression.

'Welcome back, Mr Carter. It's great to see you're finally awake. Here's a sick bowl and here's your buzzer.'

'Where am I? Is Buddy here?'

'You're in Hospital. You have lost three pints of blood and you have twenty stiches across your stomach. Not to mention that you've been in a coma for a week. Who is Buddy?'

'Buddy...he's my dog. Do you know where he is? When can I get out of here?'

'One question at a time. You're not going anywhere yet. You need plenty of rest. With the blood you've lost, you must have someone watching over you. I'll call your lady friend and let her know you're awake. She'll probably be able to tell you where your dog is. I'll be back soon to change your dressings.'

'What lady friend?' I asked.

'Lieutenant Wilkins,' the nurse said with a slight smile.

'She's not my lady friend.'

The nurse replaced her clipboard on the bed hook. 'She's been here every morning and every night to check on you. I've been around long enough to know when somebody cares.

People don't fool me easily and from what I've read, you're quite the hero. Rest up. I'll be back.'

I wondered whether it was Sarah's job to check on me or whether she genuinely cared. I looked down and saw my waist was heavily bandaged. Several parts of my arms and hands were also taped. I was in no shape to see anyone.

'Before you go, can I ask you a question?' I asked.

'Go ahead, I'm all ears,' said the nurse.

'Being romantic is not my thing. I don't want to come across as creepy. What can I say that's romantic?'

'You're asking the wrong person. I've been married for twenty years. If my husband does the dishes, that's romantic. Just tell her how you feel. You missed her, right? You think about her wherever you go? You'd like to spend more time with her?'

'Yep. That's pretty much it,' I said.

'Well tell her that. You don't have to recite Arabian poetry. There's nothing wrong with being honest. She certainly doesn't seem the type to bite your head off.'

'Ok. Thanks.'

'I'm sure you'll be fine. Anyway Curtis, you're New York's hero. Be proud of yourself. The people need someone like you. The bad news is relentless. Your story is uplifting. You're a breath of fresh air.'

I watched her leave the room, still scared shitless about expressing my feelings. My biggest fear was that Sarah wouldn't turn up.

FORTY-SIX

FEAR

Sarah received the good news. Curtis is awake. She was relieved he was alive, but she hated the visits. The hospital smelled of disinfectant and death. Visiting the hospital twice a day to check on Curtis hadn't desensitized her. It nauseated her to see people with tubes hanging out of their bodies, coughing up phlegm, and vomiting. It was worse than a murder scene.

Whenever possible she took the stairs, but today she was in a hurry. She was desperate to see Curtis.

The elevator filled with people. *Great,* she thought. *Trapped with sick people with God knows what illnesses.* Her worst fear was malfunctioning doors, her body getting caught as they closed and being decapitated when the elevator ascended. She knew it was an irrational thought, but her heart still raced.

The elevator stopped, and the doors opened to the eighth floor, opposite room number eighty-three. She hurried out and stood still for several seconds to catch her breath. Curtis's room was only two doors away and she was already wondering what to say to him. Should she hold his hand? Kiss him, or play hard to get? Maybe let him talk first? Or perhaps just a casual hug and a friendly smile?

She straightened her shirt and pushed a strand of hair behind her ear. She was determined not to let him see her vulnerability. She especially didn't want him to see she cared. She had never dreamed of falling in love with someone like Curtis. He was irresponsible and impulsive. Her heart had been broken too many times. She couldn't cope with the pain of another rejection. But the problem was, the more she convinced herself she didn't need a man, the lonelier she felt. *Damn it! He has no money, no job, and probably no future.*

Her father's words came to mind. 'Don't bother bringing home a stray dog. Find a nice Catholic boy who loves his parents and has a good job, not some lazy-ass.' She knew her father would turn in his grave if he could see her now. She loved her parents and still felt the guilt of not meeting their expectations. Her mom had wanted her to marry Harold who lived two doors away from the family. 'He's such a nice boy, Sarah. He brings me flowers and his parents never miss church.' Sarah remembered rolling her eyes, thinking that there could be nothing worse than dating the dork of the street. The thought of kissing him was vomit material.

Sarah hesitated at Curtis's door, wondering whether he also had feelings for her.

'Ok, here we go,' she whispered before entering the room.

FORTY-SEVEN

OVERCOMING EVIL

I heard a gentle knock at the door and Sarah walked towards me. I couldn't disguise my grin.

'Hi Curtis. Thank God, you're alive. You scared the living daylights out of us.'

'Sorry I didn't call, Sarah.'

She positioned herself on the edge of the bed. 'I'm relieved you're ok. By the way, do you like the lilies?' She pointed to the deep purple and yellow flowers sitting in a water pitcher on my side table.

'Very pretty, just like someone I know.' I was hoping I didn't sound too corny.

'I haven't slept since you disappeared,' Sarah admitted.

Did that mean she loved me? I wanted to hold her tight.

Sarah's cell rang. 'Yes, this is Lieutenant Wilkins. Yes, I'll pay all charges. Call me when he arrives.'

'That was a call from a county vet. A dog of yours called Buddy will be sent to the precinct this afternoon. Am I missing something here, Curtis?'

'I found him in a bad way and I wouldn't be here if it wasn't for him. I'm sorry, Sarah. You were the only person I thought could help.'

Sarah smiled. 'No need to apologize. But my apartment is

small, so you owe me big time. Maybe dinner for two would be nice.'

'It's a deal. I'd love to.'

'The name Buddy is original,' Sarah grinned.

'I was going to call him Lassie, but I thought Buddy was better. I'm just an original kind of guy.'

Sarah laughed. 'You have a sense of humor too.'

'Any news on the psychologist's victims?' I asked.

'He had a "business colleague" in Vegas. A pastor. The psychologist's clients were couriered to Vegas and delivered to the pastor's place called The Lord's House of Therapy. There, the clients were tortured and killed. Our forensic optometrist compared the reading glasses found next to the body of Linda Maloney, the commissioner's niece, to a photo of the pastor wearing glasses. It was a perfect match. Before we could get to him he'd shot himself. The bullet didn't quite finish him off. He survived and is now a paraplegic. He'll not only have his day in court, he'll be incapacitated in a wheelchair and behind bars for the rest of his life.'

'True payback,' I said.

'And that's not all. A much-respected coroner who used to work for the Clark County Coroner's Office in Vegas allegedly fell overboard on the family boat while fishing with the pastor. According to the pastor it was an accident. His body was never found and there was no evidence of foul play. Coincidentally, the coroner was replaced by a friend of the pastor's. They falsified legal documents of wealthy trustees and then bumped them off. The pastor got sloppy. The falsified documents were found at his Therapy House and the replacement coroner has a rap sheet as long as my arm.'

'Jesus, this pastor had his finger in many pies,' I said.

Sarah gave a knowing nod. 'Definitely. Our pastor was a busy villain. He was also a kingpin in the Prince Casino. He operated a major heroin trafficking ring and laundering operation, with a strip club on the side. The strip club provided his perfect hunting ground for victims. God knows how many people walked into his trap. Not surprisingly we found a collection of military automatics in his cellar. We could've had one hell of a gun battle on our hands.'

'He made it his business to know lots of important people,' I said.

Sarah grinned. 'There'll be nervous associates in Vegas hoping he doesn't rat on them and wannabe informants putting up their hand to avoid doing time. That's if they don't get bumped off in the meantime.'

'What happened to the doctor?' I asked.

'A vagrant saved your life. He shot the doctor, who was pronounced dead before he left the alleyway. I wanted the monster to have his day in court and the world to see his face and his heinous crimes. I'd hoped to hear the guilty verdict and know he'd slowly rot in a cell. I suppose the alleyway was a fitting place for him to die.' Sarah gave a deep sigh.

I held Sarah's hand. 'Thanks for checking up on me.'

'You scared the living daylights out of me, Curtis. When you went missing, I felt physically sick.'

'I'm here now. No harm done. I'm the lucky one unlike some of the doctor's victims.' I looked down with a sinking feeling. 'Do you have any other information?'

'A courier driver who transported the victims from the psychologist to the pastor in Vegas is spilling the beans about the whole operation, hoping for a lighter sentence. It was his wife who called the police about his criminal activity. Initially, she thought he was having an affair and hired a private investigator. The investigator discovered her husband had different identities. She knew nothing about her husband's secret life. He'd told her he was working for the Secret Service to protect the President!'

'What about the missing clients?' I asked Sarah, bracing

myself for the worst possible news.

'Sadly, we found a young boy's body in a walk-in freezer at the back of the pastor's House of Therapy. He's currently John Doe but hopefully, we'll be able to identify him soon. There is a blessing amongst all this evil. Sean Young, who was abducted on 5th Avenue, was rescued by the killer's wife, Magda. There was also a young girl found in the basement garage gagged and bound. I'm betting there are more victims out there. We're doing another search of Lake Mead and scouring the land at the back of the Therapy House and at his residential address.'

'So, the doctor wasn't the only killer,' I said. *Jesus.*

'The doctor was getting big money from the pastor for the deliveries. There's something else. Sorry to be the bearer of bad news but I thought it would be better coming from me than reading it in the Daily News.' Sarah paused.

'This is not sounding good,' I said.

'There was another victim, Brandy Johnson, the one who was found dead in her hospital room. According to the toxicology report, there was a high level of heroin in her bloodstream that caused her system to shut down. Although we can't prove he injected her, we managed to get surveillance footage from a parking lot adjacent to the hospital that showed the doctor entering the hospital minutes before she died. His cell's ping history also placed him a few blocks from her home.'

Sarah edged closer to me.

'You're badly injured Curtis. That means hugging could be harmful.'

'My pain has pretty well stopped now you're here,' I said.

'You're good with words, Curtis. A real Casanova.'

'Yep, that's me alright. Can I ask you something?'

'Fire away,' Sarah responded.

'Well. You see.'

'Spit it out Curtis. What is it?'

'I missed you and really want to spend time with you.'

Sarah leaned forward and stroked my face. 'I'd love to spend all day with you. We'll have to wait,' she whispered. 'I don't want you to relapse with pleasure,' she grinned.

'I'll wait. It won't be easy, but I'll definitely wait.'

Sarah gently rested her head on my shoulder. 'You better wait for me or else...'

'Or else what?' I asked.

'Or else I'll have you arrested. It'll be a house arrest. You will be confined to my place,' Sarah laughed.

'That sounds fine with me, Lieutenant. I promise I won't resist.'

There was a light tap on the door. Sarah bolted upright and straightened her hair. James entered the room.

'Hi Curtis. Good to see you're back.'

'Yeah, I'm back. This time I'm staying away from the bad guys.' Damn it. I wasn't happy to see James.

Sarah's cell rang. She looked overly anxious. 'Hi Mick, what's the latest? Ok...mm...just email me the report and I'll call you when I get back to the office.' As Sarah placed her cell in her jacket pocket, her demeanor changed. There was a concerned silence.

'Is everything ok?' I asked.

'It's Courtney.'

I could tell it was bad news. I had been hoping she wasn't the skeleton in my dream. The skeleton on the train who'd begged for my help and I'd done nothing, even when I'd found her ring in the basement.

'What about Courtney?'

'I'm sorry, Curtis, they found her body at Lake Mead not far from where the commissioner's niece was found. I'm waiting on the autopsy results.'

'If only I'd warned her. Surely, I could have said something! I was meant to find that ring and I blew it.'

'Would she have listened, Curtis?' James asked. 'She didn't

even know you, so why would she have trusted a stranger? Clients can be emotionally vulnerable and develop an attachment to their therapist.'

'Surely I could have helped in some way.'

'It's normal to want to rescue her, Curtis, but she might have gone into denial anyway,' James responded. 'Do you really think she'd have believed the only person in the world who cared for her was planning to abduct her? Courtney had no one. The psychologist knew she was easy picking. They all were. If she'd known the truth, she might have ended her life. You didn't kill her, Curtis. Ellison did.'

What he said made sense, but I still felt bad. She had slipped under the radar and now she was dead.

'You're right, but it's still sad to think she had no one,' I responded.

James continued, 'He had advertisements on YWCA noticeboards in the poorer parts of New York offering free counseling that's in a safe place. Right from the start, he portrayed himself as the good guy who cared. He would have known her self-esteem was fragile. A client can crave validation. He would have provided that and made her feel good.'

Sarah received another call. 'Yes...ok...great, thanks.' She sounded relieved. 'Janis Lang is awake and talking. We'd found her unconscious and tied up in another room at the back of the pastor's Therapy House. Her stepbrother has already been told the news and he cried with relief. Janis had a tough life. She has cutting scars on her wrist and her father suicided off the Brooklyn Bridge. Her mom told us she hoped her daughter was dead. I can't wait to give the sociopathic mom the good news her daughter is going to be ok.'

'Sounds like you guys got there just in time,' I stated.

'Yeah,' James responded. 'The evil predator is in a cage where he belongs. It's a relief to know you're in one-piece Curtis but unfortunately, I must go. I have an appointment in half an hour.' He looked at Sarah. 'Did you want to join me later for a bite to eat?'

I felt a pang of jealousy. *Please say no, Sarah.*

'Unfortunately, I've got to get back to the office for a debrief with the chief.'

I was relieved. I couldn't stand the thought of them eating together. James gave Sarah a smile before he left the room. Maybe I was reading too much into it.

My past relations had been with clingy women. Their demands had been suffocating. They'd text me a hundred times a day just because I'd fucked them. Then they called me a cold-hearted son of a bitch because I didn't want to see them again. They just didn't get it.

How I felt about Sarah was the absolute opposite. I wanted to be with her every second of every moment.

FORTY-EIGHT

WORLD VIEW

Once James left the room, Sarah sat back on the bed. 'You know, you don't have to go through this on your own, Curtis. Anytime you need to talk...'

'Thanks. I'll hold you to that. You seem to know a lot about this stuff. The police force must be an eye-opener.'

'Yeah, it can be.'

'Are you ok?' I asked.

'I hate hospitals. My sister had anorexia, so I don't have good memories.'

'No wonder. How is she now?'

Sarah looked away before replying. 'She perceived any help as criticism and thought people were constantly judging her. She wouldn't talk about it, especially to a doctor or a therapist. She denied she had a problem. If anyone bullied her on Face-book, she couldn't walk away and shrug it off. She'd help out friends when they had problems, but she couldn't help herself.'

'Do you think that started it?'

'I really don't know. I remember her punishing herself for days if she didn't get top marks at school. I couldn't understand her stress when I was happy with my passes.'

'What about your parents?' I asked.

'They kept asking why. They couldn't get answers. I've

never seen them in so much pain. Some nights I could hear my mom crying herself to sleep. My father was angry and refused to visit her in hospital. He called her a spoilt attention seeker. I'm sure he didn't mean it. He just didn't know how to cope. In the end, she passed away.'

'I'm so sorry, Sarah.'

'Don't apologize. I chose to tell you. It's normally something I keep to myself. I think the hardest thing was finding her diary after the funeral. I found it in a shoe box under her bed. She called it her self-hate diary. She'd written how much she'd hated herself and deserved to die. She said her starvation was a punishment for being alive. I can't believe how differently we viewed our lives. Now I believe *stress* is in the eye of the beholder.'

I realized there was more to Sarah than just being a tough cop. She had let me into her private world. We both leaned forward and kissed. A bomb could have hit the building without me knowing.

Sarah pulled back. 'We'd better stop before the bed catches alight.'

It was then my nurse entered the room.

'Hi Curtis, how are you feeling?' she asked.

'I couldn't feel better. When do I get out of here?'

'You need a few more days to recover. I'll give you some privacy and I'll come back to check your sutures.'

As the nurse left the room, Sarah gave me one last kiss. 'Don't worry, I'll be waiting for you. Make sure you get plenty of rest, you'll need your energy.' She winked.

FORTY-NINE

GUILT

I was discharged three days later. The world seemed a beautiful place despite returning to my roach palace. I was consumed by thoughts of Sarah. *Love does feel amazing,* I thought.

Sitting on my kitchen table was a bucket with a bottle of champagne and a note: *Darling Curtis, the commissioner has paid a month's rent in advance and he's willing to pay for any other accommodation if you wish to move. He also wants to meet the hero of New York. BTW the champagne is from me, not him, haha, love Sarah.*

Life couldn't be sweeter, I thought.

That afternoon I met Sarah at the Central Park Precinct. During all my time in New York, I'd had no idea that a precinct existed in Central Park. Our greeting was different this time. We walked into each other's arms. It felt so natural.

'Why on earth are you at this precinct of all places?'

'We received information about the Vegas pastor here so I'm just checking the paperwork and catching up with some old colleagues. What's up. I know you well enough now Curtis, that you're not here just for a friendly visit. What's on your mind?'

'I want to find out some information about a soldier called Sam Davis. She was my drill sergeant at Fort Jackson. I'd like to see her.'

'I found out you had a stint at Fort Jackson. It was unavoidable if we were going to find you,' Sarah said.

It made me a little paranoid to think Sarah knew my army history.

'Just wait here, Curtis, I'll have to check in with a colleague. I'll see what I can find out about this drill sergeant.'

Waiting was not my forte. I downed a cup of watery coffee and paced up and down the waiting room. Minutes seemed like hours.

At last, Sarah returned.

'Sorry Curtis, finding out about this sergeant took a while.'

'What have you got?'

'Sam Davis is not in the land of the living,' Sarah answered.

'What do you mean, not in the land of the living?'

'Exactly that. She now resides in the Fort Jackson Cemetery. She was killed in action three years ago while on a routine mission in Afghanistan. Her platoon was ambushed. Her K-9 military dog was also killed. Apparently, her dog was buried with her.'

I couldn't speak. I felt my eyes sting as I held back the tears. I needed to escape, to run somewhere so no one would see me.

'Is everything ok, Curtis?'

'I'm all good. Sorry, I've got to go but I'll call you. I promise.' I had to get out of the building. I couldn't believe my drill sergeant was dead. I wanted to tell her I was sorry. I wanted to thank her for saving my life.

I ended up at the other end of Central Park. I yelled out, 'How could you be dead! You're not supposed to be dead! You're supposed to be here! Why the fuck did you get yourself killed?'

Shivering, I squatted down and hid my head in my hands.

'Lookie here, it's our dog rescuer being a cry-baby. A real pussy. Hello, Mr Hero man of the neighborhood, having a little cry, are we?'

FIFTY

VINDICATION

They came out of nowhere. Jesus, what the hell was I going to do now. It was the street gang from Brooklyn. Why were they in Central Park?

'Aww, the sissy wanker has been crying.'

I wasn't going to let some teenage thugs take me out after what I'd been through. *Just focus and relax.*

'I've had a shit day man, just go on your way and no harm will be done.'

The taller boy of the group moved forward. 'You live our lives for one day then you'll know what a fuckin' shit day is,' he snarled.

Instead of helping, my words had fueled their anger. They looked hungry for violence.

'Take my wallet, take anything you want.'

They mocked me again. 'We want more than a fuckin' wallet; we want some fun.'

'I have other money; I can take you to an ATM.'

'Shut the fuck up and get your hands away from your body.'

The smallest boy looked willing. 'Hey bro, we can get some cash tonight and have some fun another time with this dumb-ass. There's no food at home, bro. Mom would be happy with us.'

'You better not fuck with us or we'll whack you, you got it? Take your jacket off and turn around, we don't want a piece pulled on us again.' They frisked me expertly.

I was their prize catch. There was no one in sight. They had the perfect opportunity to do whatever they wanted. But their desperate need for money was going to be my salvation. I'd be dead if I couldn't divert them. I had to get out of Central Park and onto a busy street.

'You've been through some bad stuff. You're all bandaged up. What is it, Mr Office Man? I say you're running from someone. Maybe you're like us,' the boy laughed.

The tallest of the three fumbled through my jacket and pulled out my wallet. He tossed it at me.

'Get your card out now.'

I slipped out the bank card. There was no more than twenty dollars in the account.

'Walk ahead and don't look behind. If you run, we'll finish you!'

I nodded. *Jesus, if I can get away from serial killers, surely, I can get away from these fuckwits.*

They followed closely behind. I was relieved to hear the traffic and the sound of hooves and carriages as we exited Central Park.

Once the ATM was in sight, the leader flashed his knife. 'Get your cash out. We'll be watching.'

They stood partially hidden from sight on a street corner. I stood in line with one person in front. I took a deep breath. This was it. I counted as if I was about to discharge a missile 5...4...3...2...1...run! I bolted across a busy intersection, weaving in and out of traffic. I was smacked by one vehicle so hard that I tumbled several times across the road. The vehicle screeched to a halt. Vehicle horns honked all around. I scrambled to my feet and charged off again. If my wounds had opened, I wasn't feeling it.

As I glanced behind, I saw a five domino-effect pileup of vehicles and the boys trying to cross between the wreckage. It held them off for only a few seconds. I couldn't believe how quickly they were onto me.

'Where the fuck has he gone! Look down there, he can't be far.'

I squeezed behind a dumpster, but not before knocking over a bottle. It gave a tinkling sound as it rolled. *Oh fuck!* I just managed to grab the tip of the bottle with my fingers. Whenever I tried to be quiet I created the loudest noise? I might as well have blown a fuckin' trumpet.

I heard footsteps rushing towards me. 'I found our man!' screamed one of the gang. 'Get the fuck out from there, little cry-baby.'

I stepped out, concealing the bottle. As one of the boys moved forward, I smashed the top of the bottle against the dumpster and sunk its jagged edge into his thigh. I wasn't going to kill street trash and end up in the pen, but I thought a good jab would do the trick.

'Got you! You fuckwit,' I yelled.

The boy screamed. 'He's stabbed me! He's stabbed me!'

The other two boys moved in. 'Let's get this pussy once and for all.'

The sound of vehicle tires screeched to a halt.

'Freeze! Police!'

Two of the boys took off, while one lay wailing in his blood.

'Place the bottle on the ground! We don't want to hurt you, just put the bottle down.'

I bent down and placed the bloodied bottle on its edge.

'Kick the bottle to us and no one else gets hurt.'

I managed to give it a side boot.

'Put your hands on the back of your head. Lie face down! Face down! Keep your hands on your head!'

I could see my side was bleeding. I gently knelt. This was

demoralizing. My life presented one fuck-up after another.

The cops wrenched my arms behind my back and I felt excruciating pain. I looked at the bloodied kid. 'Look who's the cry-baby now.'

'He's a crazy man, get him away from me!'

My fear now was trying to explain this to Sarah. I looked a bloody mess.

Back at the precinct, I sat with a cop while he checked my wounds.

'Bloody hell, Curtis, what is wrong with you?' Sarah asked.

'I've fucked up again. I'm sorry.'

'I'm not getting it. One minute we're talking normally, and the next you take off and stab some street kid. The chief is going to start wondering what I'm doing.'

I knew she was right. I knew she wanted a man, not a kid running around like a loose cannon.

'I really want to trust you. I'm over the bad boys.'

'I was pounced on by street kids from Brooklyn. It was self-defense. They would have killed me.' I hoped I didn't sound lame.

'I can get them for assault if that's the case,' Sarah responded.

'I don't want to press charges. Do you think the commissioner could pull some strings to get them some work? Maybe they could do community service at an...animal shelter. I'm guessing their life has been shit. It might stop them ending up in the pen and having criminal role models teaching them the tricks of their trade.'

'Gee Curtis, you're sounding like a street cop. I'm sure the chief will agree to redirect them. I can arrange a referral for a multisystemic therapy program.'

'I'm not sure what that is but thanks,' I said.

'It's a service for juvenile offenders. They help out their families, their schooling and get them into community work.' Sarah's voice softened. 'That's a change of heart, Curtis. No doubt about it, you're full of surprises.'

'I'm also wanting to thank the vagrant for saving my life. I'm not sure how I can meet up with him.'

Sarah nodded. 'I can organize that for you. There's more to this vagrant than meets the eye. A driver high on carfentanil ploughed into his vehicle, killing his wife and two children. He survived with the family dog. He's been living on the streets ever since.'

'Jesus! His whole family wiped out in seconds! What's this drug carfentanil?' I asked.

'It's a synthetic drug that's cheap to buy. Just getting that stuff on your skin is an express lane to the morgue. It would be a dream chemical for a psychopathic leader. Their enemy would drop like flies.'

'Yeah, that's evil shit.' There was a momentary silence, then, my thoughts switched from evil to good. 'Who'll be interviewing the vagrant?' I asked.

'Don't worry, it's going to be me, and I'll look after him. The chief is organizing accommodation for him and arranging a reward with the commissioner. I've organized trauma counseling and he's willing to do it. I've also arranged a vet check for his dog.'

'Thanks for looking after them,' I said.

'I don't mind. The poor guy has experienced a real-life horror story,' Sarah replied.

'There is one other thing Sarah and I promise I won't ask for anything else.'

'Yes, Curtis?' Sarah responded with raised eyebrows and a slight grin.

'I'm going to South Carolina tomorrow to visit the Fort Jackson Cemetery. Would you be able to drive me? Buddy may not be keen on a flight. I promise, I owe you big time. Maybe a vacation together once my reward money comes through and I pay off the mafia?'

'It's a deal. I'm betting it's to do with this drill sergeant but in the meantime, I'll call a cab to take you to the doctor's. You're not looking in great shape. South Carolina is a long drive, so you better have plenty of rest. I'll pick you up at 6.00 am. Buddy can have the back seat.'

'How's he going in your apartment.'

'Well, he didn't take long to settle in. He's already claimed my couch as his bed. He sleeps on his back with his legs in the air. He looks like he's in heaven. I've always been a cat person, but I must admit, I'm growing fond of him.'

I leaned over and whispered in her ear. 'Cops aren't too bad after all, especially when they're as kind and sexy as you.'

Sarah grinned. 'Stop it Curtis, sucking up will get you nowhere. Anyway, you'll ruin my tough cop reputation.'

FIFTY-ONE

THE COMMON GOOD

Sarah called exactly on 6.00 am. 'I'm out the front in the vehicle with Buddy,' Sarah said.

I looked down onto the street and saw Buddy's head poking out the rear window. Buddy looked up and gave two demanding barks. He hadn't forgotten me!

I raced out of the apartment block, my wounds forgotten, not before giving little mouse Charlie his breakfast. Outside, the cool air brushed my face. The air smelled sweeter and the sky was clear.

Buddy leapt from the vehicle window and into my arms. His coat was shiny, and his black tail was bushy. The only sign of his injuries was a shaved neck where his wound had been stitched.

Sarah called out. 'Hop in, Curtis. I'm waiting for a hug too.'

'I usually don't obey orders, but this is definitely an exception,' I replied.

Her lips were warm and welcoming.

'Now let's get going or we'll be arrested for sexual misconduct and Fort Jackson is a full day's drive.'

'Do you know any more about this drill sergeant?' I asked.

'Only that the sergeant and her military dog Hugo were both awarded the highest US Army bravery medals.'

'Are you ok, Curtis?'

'I'm good,' I replied but part of me felt bad.

'I've heard that before. I'm a good listener if you want to talk,' Sarah replied.

I filled Sarah in on some of the blanks in my life. She was right. She was a good listener and I'd felt better for it. When we arrived, I noticed the cemetery had changed in size. There were many more headstones. The last time I'd stood here the world had owed me and people were assholes.

'Here's a map of the cemetery. It's divided into four sections. Your drill sergeant is in section two.'

'Where did you manage to find this?' I asked.

'It was easy. I did a search of her name on the 'Find a Grave' website.' Sarah pointed to the map. 'Here's the section and the site number.'

'I don't know how to thank you.'

Sarah grinned. 'Don't worry, I'll think of something tonight. You better hurry before it gets dark. Do you need company?' she asked.

I didn't want to reject Sarah's kindness but at the same time I needed to be alone. 'I'll be ok, but thanks for the offer.'

I turned to Buddy. 'See that sign there? It states pets are not allowed on the cemetery grounds at any time. Sorry Buddy, you're staying right here with Sarah.'

Buddy gave a sharp short bark and as I left the parking lot, Sarah called out.

'Curtis...wait. Don't you think Buddy could have a quick visit? After all, he's a hero too.'

She was right. It wouldn't be fair if we couldn't both thank the sergeant. 'C'mon, Buddy! C'mon boy!'

He was at my feet in seconds.

'You be good or we'll both be kicked out.'

I followed Sarah's map and headed for the spot marked 'Section B'.

Turning the corner, I was struck by the sight of hundreds

of gravestones. They looked like giant white teeth, stretching across the field in even rows, upright like a platoon of soldiers waiting for their marching orders.

We made our way through the rows of headstones. I noticed one soldier was only eighteen. My heart sank. I couldn't help but feel like shit for being alive.

Buddy suddenly changed direction and sat purposefully at a gravestone. It was the sergeant's. *How the hell did he know?*

The sad irony of it hurt. One day I was pissing on her boots; the next I was thanking her for saving my life.

Suddenly, the sound of distant gunfire broke the silence. The shots of a three-volley salute echoed through neighboring pines followed by the haunting refrain of a bugle. Figures could be seen dotted on the horizon. It wasn't a day of celebration. I noticed a burial ceremony in the distance. I wondered how it was possible to walk away from someone you loved who was six feet under. *Nothing stays the same,* I thought.

I looked at the words etched in the white sandstone: *Together in life, together in death. May God be with them on their final journey.*

'I was an asshole. Your survival training saved my life.' I stood by the headstone and gave a salute of respect.

I wished my drill sergeant could feel the breeze and experience the sweet smell of pine. I stood in silence and resisted the urge to wallow in self-pity.

I turned around. Buddy was gone. I looked up and noticed he was sitting by the pines.

'C'mon boy.' The last thing I needed was a cemetery violation.

As Buddy dashed back, I saw Sarah standing several yards away.

I hurried to her and held her close. Dark clouds rolled across the fields, their moving shadows reflecting off the white headstones.

'We'd better get back to the vehicle before it rains. By the way, who was the soldier standing by the pines?' Sarah asked.

'What soldier?'

'She shook Buddy's paw,' Sarah said.

'Beats me.' I hadn't seen my sergeant, but I'd felt her presence.

'There's something I've been meaning to tell you, Curtis.'

'You have me worried.'

'It's nothing bad. It's just that...as you know...I've been wanting to change careers and I've been offered a job in California working for the SPCA. I can work at home and on site. Like I told you a while ago, working with animals is something I've wanted to do for a long time. It's a drop-in pay but I'm ready for a sea change. There's also a part-time job available in Monterey working for a conservation organization.'

'They must be special to get your attention,' I said.

'Yes, they are,' Sarah responded. 'I hadn't heard of them until I came across their Facebook page. One day, I'd like to be an environmental advocate against these big oil and gas companies. They love to fill politicians' pockets with dirty energy money while our world is heating up. Besides that, life is too short. It can go in a flash. I don't want to be waking up in a nursing home and wondering why I'd stayed in a rut.'

'If that's what you want to do, then go for it. It's great you want to do something you believe in. I'm sure the oil and gas companies will be a pushover with your experience in the NYPD. I'm happy for you.' But I was devastated. Did this mean, 'goodbye Curtis it was nice knowing you, it's not you it's me? I'm off to save the planet but you're not included.' Before I could feel any worse, Sarah continued.

'There's a timber home for sale in Sand City. It's not far from the beach. The only problem is, it's too big for one person and it would feel lonely without you. I'm wondering whether you'd be interested in a Californian lifestyle. Of course, not forgetting Buddy. I'm sure he'd love the walks on the beach.'

I exhaled with relief. 'Well then, I'd better start looking for work in California.'

'Does that mean yes?' Sarah asked.

'Definitely. Once I've paid the mafia and they're off my back, I'll be packing my bags. What do you think Buddy?'

Buddy gave two rapid barks. His bushy tail wagged in the breeze.

I grinned. 'And it's a yes from him.'

I couldn't think of a better beginning.